GiRLS'
NiGHT OUT

"Saved by the Bell" titles include:

Mark-Paul Gosselaar: Ultimate Gold

Mario Lopez: High-Voltage Star

Behind the Scenes at "Saved by the Bell"

Beauty and Fitness with "Saved by the Bell"

▲ ▼ ▲

Hot new fiction titles:

Zack Strikes Back

Bayside Madness

California Scheming

Girls' Night Out

Zack's Last Scam

Class Trip Chaos

GIRLS' NIGHT OUT

by Beth Cruise

Collier Books
Macmillan Publishing Company
New York

Maxwell Macmillan Canada
Toronto

Maxwell Macmillan International
New York   Oxford   Singapore   Sydney

To
all the gang
down at the Max

Collier Books   Maxwell Macmillan Canada, Inc.
Macmillan Publishing Company   1200 Eglinton Avenue East
866 Third Avenue   Suite 200
New York, NY 10022   Don Mills, Ontario M3C 3N1

Macmillan Publishing Company is part of the Maxwell
Communication Group of Companies.

First Collier Books edition 1992
Printed in the United States of America

10 9 8 7 6 5 4 3 2

Library of Congress Cataloging-in-Publication Data
Cruise, Beth.
Girls' night out / by Beth Cruise. — 1st Collier Books
ed.
p.   cm.
Summary: Zack and the rest of the gang worry when
Jessie tries to change her image by dating a surfer
named Thunder, whose scheming ex-girlfriend keeps
turning up.
ISBN 0-02-042766-2
[1.   Interpersonal relations—Fiction.   2. Self-
perception—Fiction.]   I. Title.
PZ7.C88827Gi   1992
[Fic]—dc20   92-24648

Chapter 1

▲ ▼ ▲ ▼ ▲ ▼ ▲

The door to the principal's office closed with a slam behind Zack Morris. Zack checked to make sure he still had his fingers.

"Touchy, touchy, Mr. Belding," he murmured to the closed door.

Mr. Belding must be having a bad day. Why else would he hit the roof when he heard about Zack's proposal for his science project? Everyone else in the class thought it would be awesome to turn the school swimming pool into a shark aquarium. It was only for a weekend, and Zack had already gotten the swim team's okay. Mr. Belding just had no respect for learning. Or else he wasn't a fish lover.

Just a minor setback, Zack reassured himself. He was still the guy who kept Bayside High on its toes. As he passed the glass doors of the cafeteria, Zack peered at his reflection. Smoothing back his blond hair, he lifted one eyebrow tantalizingly and flashed his devilish grin. No doubt about it. He still had the right stuff.

Now all he needed was the girl who kept Bayside rocking and rolling: Kelly Kapowski, the prettiest, sweetest, cutest girl in the senior class, not to mention the best cheerleader Bayside High had ever seen. Just because Kelly had recently become his girlfriend again didn't mean Zack was prejudiced. He'd thought she was all those things when he was chasing her, too.

Ahead of him, Zack saw his friend Lisa Turtle heading for her locker. It was probably time for a makeup check. Lisa was a naturally gorgeous African-American teen, but she believed that no girl should ever dream that mascara isn't an absolute necessity of life.

"Hey, Lisa," Zack greeted her. "What's up besides the cheerleaders' hemlines since I talked them into those new uniforms?"

"The usual," Lisa said. "Screech turned his face green in chemistry class today."

Zack grinned. Samuel "Screech" Powers could always be counted on to turn a dull day around. "Hmmmm. Was that a forest green or a lime green?"

Lisa thought a minute. "Puce," she decided.

"Hey, guys!" Kelly Kapowski rounded the corner, her long, shiny dark hair bouncing and her deep blue eyes sparkling. "Did you hear the news?" she asked as she came up to them.

"Sure," Zack said. "Lisa says it's puce."

Kelly frowned. "I thought it was bronze."

Lisa nodded thoughtfully. "Maybe. If the bronze is really, really old and gets that gunky green color."

"But it's brand-new!" Kelly exclaimed.

"Since sixth period," Lisa agreed.

"I thought it happened just now," Kelly said, puzzled.

"Was there a lot of smoke?" Zack said. "There was last time."

"Smoke?" Kelly asked. "You know there's no smoking at Bayside. And Jessie doesn't smoke."

"Jessie was there, too?" Lisa squeaked. "What does *her* face look like?"

Jessie Spano was their other best friend. She was senior class president, not to mention on the honor roll every semester, but they liked her anyway.

"Her face?" Kelly asked. "Proud, I guess."

"Proud to be green?" Zack guffawed. "Now, I call that supreme dedication to science."

"It wasn't science, it was history," Kelly said impatiently. "What are you guys talking about, anyway?"

"Screech turning his face green in chemistry class," Lisa said. "Isn't that what *you're* talking about?"

Kelly blew out an exasperated breath. "I'm talking about Jessie! Her face isn't green!"

Just then, A. C. Slater, Jessie's boyfriend, came up to them. "Screech turned Jessie's face green? Let me at that guy. I'll introduce his face to my fist." Slater flexed an impressive muscle, but his warm brown eyes were dancing. Everybody knew he was just kidding. Slater might have the biggest muscles in school, but his heart was made of mush, and everybody knew it.

"Calm down, Slater," Kelly said with a giggle. "We got our wires crossed. I was trying to tell everyone that Jessie won the history medal."

Everyone sighed. "I thought it was something *important*," Zack said.

Lisa reached into her locker for her jacket. "It's not exactly a news flash, Kelly. Jessie wins *all* the academic medals."

"Incredible that such brains could be crammed into such curves," Slater said. "And don't tell Jessie I said that."

Slater and Jessie were crazy about each other, but they didn't like to tell each other that fact very often. The gang swore that they liked to fight just as much as they liked to make up.

"You guys have been going steady for over a month now," Lisa calculated. "This is definitely a record."

Slater winced. "Don't say it out loud. You might jinx it. We haven't had a fight in a week." Just then, his eye was caught by a pretty blond girl strolling by. "There's Tamara Talbot. I've got to ask her if I can borrow her history notes. I fell asleep this morning in class. A date with Jessie always tires me out. My mouth really gets a workout."

"From kissing?" Lisa asked with a giggle.

"You got it," Slater said with a smile. He hurried off after Tamara.

Screech walked up as Slater left. His face was a pale shade of sickly green underneath his wild curls. The green clashed with the patterned shirt he was wearing and with the orange suspenders holding up his lilac-checked pants. But Screech's fashion sense was nothing compared to his crazily illogical brain.

Zack peered at him. "Definitely puce," he told Lisa.

Lisa studied Screech's face. "The funny thing is, he doesn't look any different."

"Thank you, Lisa," Screech said with a deep sigh. "You always say the right thing." Screech had worshiped Lisa from afar since grade school. As for Lisa, she always said that she wished he'd worship her from someplace *truly* far away—like Alaska.

Just then, Jessie Spano strode toward them on long denim legs, her mane of brown curls flying. Her pretty hazel eyes were shining. "Guess what!" she announced.

"We heard," Zack said.

"Congratulations, Jessie," Lisa said. "It's never a surprise, but it's always an honor."

"You deserve it," Kelly told her. "You've worked really hard this year."

"Where's Slater?" Jessie asked, looking around the busy hallway. "I want to tell him the news."

"He went to the gym, I think," Zack said quickly. If Jessie saw Slater talking to Tamara, who knew what could happen? Jessie had a hot temper, and Slater was a terrible flirt. Their chemistry was positively combustible. Now, *there* was an idea for a science project! *Too dangerous*, Zack decided. He'd end up looking more scorched than Screech.

"Maybe Slater's in the cafeteria," Lisa said helpfully.

But it didn't do any good. The gang saw Jessie's eyes narrow as she caught sight of Slater. With a sinking feeling, Zack turned around.

Dressed in a short, red miniskirt and boots, Tamara Talbot was leaning against her locker while Slater, his back to them, leaned on one arm on the locker next to her. Tamara smiled up into Slater's face worshipfully, as though he were the quarterback who'd scored the winning touchdown in the big game. As a matter of fact, he *was* the quarterback who'd scored the winning touchdown in last Saturday's game.

Jessie definitely had some tough competition. All the girls at Bayside High swooned over Slater. And he didn't mind it one bit, especially if the girl was as pretty as Tamara.

"I can see he's *very* busy," Jessie said icily.

"He wanted to borrow her history notes," Kelly said quickly.

Slater turned and saw Jessie. For a minute, an uneasy expression crossed his face, but it was replaced with his easygoing grin. He said good-bye to Tamara and ambled toward the group.

"Hey, babe," he said, greeting Jessie. "On the absolutely gorgeous scale, I'd say you were hitting a solid ten today."

Jessie crossed her arms. "Oh? And where would Tamara Talbot fall on the scale?"

Slater grinned. "Nine and a half. She just doesn't have your smile." Jessie continued to frown at him, and Slater's grin faltered. "Not that I could tell right now," he added.

"Maybe you should go back and talk to Tamara, then," Jessie said. "She had *no* trouble smiling at you."

Slater sighed. "Not this again."

Jessie tossed her head, her curls flying. "What's that, Slater?"

"The green-eyed monster," Slater said. "You're jealous."

"When you go out with the biggest flirt in Bayside High, it goes with the territory," Jessie snapped.

"Maybe you should try trusting me," Slater shot back. "Trust is the basis of any mature relationship, Jessie."

"I agree," Screech said, nodding. "I trust Lisa completely."

"We don't *have* a relationship, Screech," Lisa pointed out. "And if we ever do, point out the way to the nearest cliff."

Jessie didn't even blink. She was still hopping mad, and even Lisa and Screech's sparring wouldn't slow her down. "Mature?" she said, her eyes flashing fire. "I'm supposed to listen to lectures on *maturity* from the guy who likes to stick straws up his nose?"

"Excuse me," Slater said. "I forgot for a second that you didn't have a sense of humor. Everybody else *loves* my rhinoceros impersonation."

"Are you sure you need the straws, Slater?" Jessie shot back. "If you really want a laugh, you can just be yourself."

Slater crossed his muscular arms. "You know, Jessie," he said softly, "you go too far sometimes. Maybe you could learn a thing or two from girls like Tamara."

Jessie crossed her arms, too, and they faced each other like members of the All-Star Debating Team.

Lisa rolled her eyes. "Here we go again," she said. "I should sell the rights to the Spano-Slater matches to cable TV. I'd make a million dollars."

"Learn from Tamara?" Jessie asked. "Let me see. What could I learn? Giggling lessons? How to say, 'Wow. Really?' to whatever a guy says? How to buy the tightest possible jeans without cutting off your circulation?"

"Try this," Slater said, taking a step toward Jessie. "Making a guy feel like he's special. Not putting him down. Maybe even flattering him a little bit, just to make him feel good. Treating him like he's smart."

"That should be easy for Tamara," Jessie said scornfully. "I've met logs with bigger IQs."

"It doesn't take a big IQ to know how to treat a guy," Slater countered. "You don't know *everything*, Jessie. You can win every academic medal at school, but that won't change the fact that there's large gaps in your education when it comes to making a guy happy."

Jessie drew in her breath sharply, and tears sprang to her eyes. She quickly turned her head so that no one would see them. Tossing her curls over her shoulder, she reached over and grabbed her jacket from her locker.

"Fine," she said, turning back again. "If you like the way Tamara treats you, maybe she'll treat you to a date."

"I'm sure she will if I ask her," Slater said, his voice low and dangerous.

Jessie shrugged. "So ask her."

"Maybe I will."

"Maybe you should."

"Hey, you guys," Kelly said nervously. "Don't do this. Let's all cool it."

"Yeah," Zack chimed in quickly. "And I know just what will do it. Rocky Road ice-cream sundaes at the Max." The Max was the Bayside High hang-out and the gang's favorite place to settle down with serious junk food.

"*Cooling it* is a great idea," Jessie said. "And I think I'll start with this relationship!" She looked at Kelly and Lisa. "I have a meeting now, but I'll see you guys later, right?"

"We'll go with you," Lisa said. "Kelly and I have to stop off at the gym for a cheerleader meeting."

The girls took off, and Zack heard Slater groan. His mouth had dropped open, and his face was pale. "I just remembered something. Something horrible's going to happen!"

"What?" Screech asked. "Did the Max take Rocky Road ice cream off the menu?"

"Worse," Slater croaked.

"Oh, no!" Screech wailed. "Not pistachio!"

"Worse." Slater looked at them, his face full of doom. He pronounced the words that struck terror into every guy's heart.

"It's girls' night out," he said.

Chapter 2

▲ ▽ ▲ ▽ ▲ ▽ ▲

Zack gulped and looked at Slater. "Oh, man," he moaned. "Tonight?"

"Jessie's mom is going to San Diego this weekend," Slater explained. "She gave Jessie permission to have Kelly and Lisa sleep over. Three girls and *no curfew*."

"Sounds like fun," Screech said brightly.

Slater gave him a sour look. "Think, Screech. Imagine what trouble those three could get into. And one of them is very, very mad at me."

"Trust," Screech said. "Remember, Slater? Trust is the basis of any mature relationship."

"Right," Zack said. "So I'm not worried. I trust Kelly completely."

"I trust Lisa completely," Screech said.

"You're not *dating* Lisa," Zack reminded him.

"That's why it's so easy," Screech responded logically.

"I trust Kelly and Lisa, too," Slater said with a groan. "It's *Jessie* I'm worried about."

Sunk in gloom, the three guys looked at the empty space where the three girls had been. Finally Slater sighed.

"What do I care?" he said with a shrug. "Jessie said no strings, right? So do you guys want to grab a pizza and a movie tonight? I don't feel like hanging out at home, that's for sure."

"Sorry, Slater," Zack said. "I can't. I promised to baby-sit for my nephew. It's my older sister's wedding anniversary, and she and her husband haven't been out alone for ages."

"And I've got another chemistry experiment to do," Screech said. "I've got to figure out how to get my face back to normal." He rubbed his puce-colored face thoughtfully.

Zack eyed Screech's rubbery features. "Normal? Good luck, Screech."

"Catch you guys later, then," Slater said.

"Later," Zack echoed. He headed off down the hall thoughtfully. Just because Kelly attracted guys like bees to honey didn't mean he should worry. Kelly would be true to him. He trusted her. He did.

Still, Zack thought, *I've never been fond of bee stings.* . . .

▲   ▼   ▲

That night after dinner, Slater took a big slice of chocolate cake and a glass of milk to his room. He usually ate dessert at the table with his parents, but his mother had suddenly bolted from the table in the middle of dinner. She'd been spooning up the mashed potatoes when his father brought the swordfish in from the grill, and suddenly, she'd just run out.

Slater asked his father what was wrong, but his father just said that his mom wasn't feeling well. They ate dinner in silence, and then his father went off to talk to his mother in the bedroom.

Slater could hear them now, talking in low voices behind closed doors. He couldn't hear what they were saying, but it sounded pretty intense. He turned on the TV. He didn't want to hear anything. Whatever it was, it couldn't be good.

He swallowed a bite of chocolate cake, but it tasted like sawdust. He was worried. Things had been definitely weird around the house lately. His mother looked unhappy, and she dragged around the house like a limp rag. Usually she was full of life and energy, singing and cracking jokes and playing tennis and cooking and going off to work with a big smile on her face. Now she looked as green as Screech did.

Slater pushed the cake away and stared out the window. His parents were having problems, he could feel it. What if they were talking about a divorce? Lots of kids' parents got divorced these days. Jessie's father lived way off in San Francisco. For the first time, Slater really understood how hard that must be for Jessie. He'd really miss his dad if he moved out.

Jessie. She was the perfect person to talk to about this. When things got serious, she cut out the wisecracks and really listened. Why did he have to pick a fight with her, today of all days? And tonight she'd probably go out and meet someone else. Someone who *didn't* pick fights with her. Someone who wasn't a macho jerk like him.

Slater jumped up. "No way," he said out loud. There had to be something he could do.

▲   ▼   ▲

Zack angled his chair just right. He placed the plate of sandwiches by his elbow and reached for his binoculars. He took a big bite of his favorite sandwich—egg salad with bacon, lettuce, and to-mato—and looked through the binoculars.

Darn! What was the matter with people, any-way! How rude of Jessie to keep her curtains closed!

Zack lowered the binoculars. Did it mean she had something to hide? What were they *doing* over there, anyway? Did they have to pull the curtains if they were just sitting around listening to music or watching TV? The curtains in front of the sliding glass doors on the family room were never closed. What was going on?

Zack stood up. Trust was important, sure. But never underestimate what a little spying can do to even things out.

▲   ▼   ▲

Jessie crossed her legs and leaned forward to lock eyes with Kelly and Lisa. "I have something super-important to discuss with you. It's about my newest campaign."

"Who do you want to save now?" Lisa asked, taking a handful of popcorn. "Let us guess. Baby seals?"

"Baby seals were freshman year," Kelly said. "My turn. Dolphins?"

"Kelly, really," Lisa said, rolling her eyes. "That's old news. Remember last spring when Jessie was tearing our tuna sandwiches out of our hands and stomping on them?"

Kelly laughed. "Screech liked them better that way. How about birds?"

"Condors?" Lisa guessed.

"You guys—" Jessie tried.

"Bald eagles?" Kelly asked.

Lisa giggled. "She'll start a campaign to buy them all toupees."

Lisa and Kelly burst out laughing.

"Okay, cut it out, you guys," Jessie said. "What I'm talking about is—"

"Maybe we should move on to rodents," Kelly said with a giggle. "Marsh rats?"

"Leave it to Jessie to want to save rats," Lisa said, rolling her eyes. "Okay, I vote for marsh rats."

"Unless—" Kelly mused.

"*You guys!*" Jessie yelled. "I'm not talking about saving *anything*. Or maybe I am," she said more quietly. "Myself."

That got Kelly and Lisa's attention. "You?" Lisa asked, surprised. "Jessie Spano as an endangered species?"

"What do you mean?" Kelly asked.

"I mean that my newest campaign is to learn how to be a girl," Jessie said in a small voice.

"Gee, Jessie," Kelly said. "I think you have that one covered."

Jessie wiggled impatiently. "No, I mean a *girl* girl. You know, the type guys really go for. I want to learn the right clothes to wear. I want to learn how to giggle. I want to learn how to flirt."

Kelly and Lisa exchanged glances. "You want to learn how to *giggle*?" Lisa asked doubtfully.

Jessie nodded. "I want to learn how to be dumb. Can you guys teach me?"

"Gee, thanks," Kelly said.

"I didn't mean it that way," Jessie said quickly. "But, Kelly, you and Lisa know how to talk to guys.

You don't lecture them or talk about serious things. You laugh at their jokes. Half the time, I don't think that guys are funny."

"They're not," Lisa said. "But you laugh anyway."

Jessie smacked her knee for emphasis. "You see? That's what I'm talking about. You *know* these things, Lisa. Now, the first thing I want to do is take shopping lessons from you."

"That's silly," Lisa said. But then she thought for a minute. "That means some extra trips to the mall. Sure, Jessie, I'd be glad to."

Jessie turned to Kelly. "And I'm thinking about trying out for the cheerleading team. Could you give me some pointers?"

"You *hate* cheerleading, Jessie," Kelly argued. "You said on your radio show that it was out of the sexist Dark Ages. Just an excuse for guys to look at girls in miniskirts."

"That reminds me," Jessie said. She opened a notebook by her knee and scribbled something in it. "I have to take up the hems on all my skirts. They're not short enough."

Kelly looked at Lisa worriedly. Jessie was acting really weird. Obviously, Slater's taunts today had hit home. But he hadn't been serious. Everyone knew that Slater loved Jessie just the way she was. They all did.

"I know what you guys are thinking," Jessie said

defensively. "And this has nothing to do with what Slater said. I've been thinking about it for a while."

"You have?" Kelly asked.

"Well, since this afternoon," Jessie admitted. "So far this year, I've instituted the recycling plan at school. I was the chairperson of the Green Teens Great Park Cleanup, and I organized the Campaign to Save the Yellow-Breasted Migratory Waterfowl. Not to mention busting my boots on schoolwork. Why can't I have a little *fun* for a change?"

"There's nothing wrong with fun," Lisa agreed.

"I'm all for it," Kelly said.

Jessie leaned closer, and her hazel eyes sparkled with mischief. "Good. Because I want to start tonight!"

▲　　　▼　　　▲

Zack crawled along the side of the Spano house. A branch from a bush whacked him in the face, and a sharp rock poked his palm, but he kept on going.

He could see light streaming out from between the curtains in the family room. If he got close enough, he could peek in. He had to know what was going on!

Zack inched closer. When he got to the doors, he kept behind the curtains and slowly peeked in the gap.

Relief flooded through him when he saw that the girls were alone. Kelly, looking adorable in curlers, was munching on some popcorn. Lisa was polishing her toenails. And Jessie was trying on makeup. A typical girls' slumber party. Nothing to worry about. He could go home.

Stealthily, Zack began to crawl backward. His hand came down on something warm and squishy. He yelped in surprise. Then he looked down and discovered that it was Slater's foot.

"What are *you* doing here?" Zack demanded.

"Shhhh," Slater hissed. "Do you want them to hear us?"

Just then, they heard the sound of one of the sliding glass doors opening. They stared at each other in horror, then leaped behind the bushes bordering the house. Their heads met with a crack as they landed.

"Oww," Zack moaned, but Slater put his hand on the back of Zack's head and pushed him down to shut him up.

Jessie stuck her head out of the door. "Domino?" she called. Domino was Jessie's dalmation. "Is that you?"

An answering bark came from inside the house. Jessie shrugged and went back inside, sliding the door shut behind her.

Zack spat the dirt out of his mouth. "Thanks, Slater," he said. "But I already had dinner."

"Sorry, preppy," Slater said. "But if Jessie had seen us, we'd be *Domino's* dinner."

"What are you doing here, anyway?" Zack asked crossly.

Slater grinned. "I remembered that you don't *have* an older sister. So how could you have a nephew?"

"So sue me," Zack grumbled. "You're the one who made me paranoid. And it was all for nothing. It's just a typical toenail-polishing party."

"Good," Slater said. "But I just want to see for myself." He crawled toward the glass doors and peeked in. When he crawled backward again, his hand hit something soft and squishy, and then that something gave a strangled yelp. Slater jumped up and almost knocked heads with Screech.

They heard quick footsteps heading for the sliding glass doors, and Slater and Screech leaped over the bushes and landed with a crash on Zack, who let out another "Oof." But before Slater could push his face into the dirt again, Zack elbowed him, and Slater let out an even bigger "Yeow."

"Who's there?" Jessie said. She scanned the darkness anxiously.

Lisa came up and stood right behind her. "It sounded like someone was strangling a cat."

Jessie turned away. "Nobody's out here. Let's forget about it. It's time to get ready. We have a superbig night ahead!"

The door slid shut again. The three guys exchanged glances.

"A big night?" Zack whispered. "What do they mean, a big night?"

"I don't know," Slater said. "But it's none of our business."

"Right," Zack said.

Screech nodded. "Right. If the girls want to go out and have a wild time with other guys, it's their prerogative."

Zack and Slater looked at each other.

"I mean, what are you going to do, follow them all over Palisades?" Screech went on.

Zack and Slater smiled.

"We can take my car," Zack said.

Chapter 3

▲ ▼ ▲ ▼ ▲ ▼ ▲

Zack dashed back home to get his car keys. On the way out the door, he grabbed three baseball caps. It might help disguise their faces. He backed the Mustang out of his driveway and parked it a little bit down the street from Jessie's house. Slater and Screech dashed out of the shadows of Jessie's side yard and jumped in. The three guys hunched down in their seats and waited.

They were just in time. In another moment, the girls spilled out of the house and ran for Jessie's car. They each looked gorgeous, with bouncy, shining hair, short miniskirts, and expectant looks on their faces.

"I wish they didn't look so *happy*," Zack groaned as he started the engine and followed Jessie through the streets of Palisades.

"They're heading for the beach," Slater observed after a few minutes.

So was everybody else in Palisades on this balmy, gorgeous evening. Jessie drove slowly up Ocean Boulevard with all the windows down. Lisa and Kelly were in the front seat with her, and the three girls waved and smiled as the car was followed by honks and whistles.

Zack frowned as he saw Kelly laughing as a guy on the sidewalk got down on his knees and blew her a kiss. "I'm never letting her out of my sight again," he muttered.

As they traveled farther up the coast, the traffic suddenly got worse.

"What's going on?" Zack fretted. "I'm going to lose them."

"I know where they're going!" Screech suddenly burst out. "There's a carnival on the pier tonight. They have rides and booths set up where you can win stuffed animals. Now we know why Jessie said they were headed for a big night out. They probably want to win stuffed animals. Maybe they're redecorating their rooms."

Zack rolled his eyes at Slater. Somehow, they didn't think the girls were heading for the pier to cuddle up to teddy bears.

Soon Jessie found a parking space. Zack eased into one a block farther down. The guys pulled their caps down over their faces and kept the girls in sight as they headed for the pier. It seemed like every teen in the Los Angeles area was headed there, too. And every single guy swiveled and took a second look at Jessie, Lisa, and Kelly.

Slater looked grim. "Just let any of those guys try to hit on Jessie. I'll be hitting on *him*."

"Trust is what it's all about, Slater," Screech told him earnestly.

Slater cocked an eyebrow at him. "How would you like a moonlight swim, Screech? I can arrange one." He pointed to the dark water way down below.

"I didn't bring my suit," Screech said. "But thanks, anyway, pal."

Suddenly Lisa turned around to check out a display of straw hats. Zack grabbed Slater's and Screech's elbows and whirled them around. They pretended to study the menu at the hot dog stand.

"Whew," Zack said.

"That was close," Slater breathed.

"I'll say," Screech piped up. "We almost passed the stand, and I'm hungry. Chili dogs all around?"

"C'mon," Slater said. "They're headed for the target shooting."

"Cheeseburgers?" Screech tried.

"Let's give them a minute," Zack said nervously. "Pizza?"

His eyes on Jessie, Slater sighed. "Wow, momma. What a hot tamale."

Still scrutinizing the menu, Screech shook his head. "No tamales, Slater. But they do have tacos!"

Slater rolled his eyes. "You are definitely going to be swimming with the fishes tonight, fella."

"Did you say fish? They have fried clams," Screech said. "I just hope they have tartar sauce."

Zack sighed and leaned against the refreshment booth. "I have a feeling it's going to be a long night," he said.

▲   ▼   ▲

It felt *good* to be out on her own, Jessie decided. The full moon silvered the dark ocean, and a warm breeze caressed her bare arms. Stars were starting to twinkle overhead. Normally she'd be thinking about Slater, about how nice it would be to share a night like this with him. But tonight, it felt good just to be free.

Jessie's gaze traveled aimlessly over the group of kids leaning against the pier railing. With a shock, she met a pair of hypnotic eyes staring deeply into hers. Blushing deeply, Jessie jerked her head away.

"There's a guy over there staring at me," she murmured to the girls.

"So?" Lisa said. "This is your chance, Jessie. Stare back."

"Stare back? But—"

"No buts," Lisa said firmly. "Didn't you say that tonight you were going to flirt like mad?"

"I did," Jessie admitted. "But I was sitting in my nice, safe family room at the time."

"C'mon, Jessie," Kelly urged. "Go for it."

Jessie peeked over at the pier railing again. The guy was still staring at her. And he was *gorgeous*. He had long, shiny blond hair and a terrific body. Jessie felt herself blushing again, but instead of turning away, she smiled. He smiled back.

She jerked her head away. "He smiled at me," she hissed.

"That's the idea, girlfriend," Lisa advised. "Which one is he? We have to check him out."

"Over by the railing," Jessie muttered. "Blond hair. White jeans. Blue tank top."

Kelly and Lisa turned casually, as if they were going to scan the horizon.

"You've got to be kidding," Kelly said.

"No way," Lisa sputtered.

"What's wrong with him?" Jessie asked.

"Ab-so-lute-ly nothing, honey," Lisa drawled.

"But he isn't your type," Kelly said. "He's a . . . a surfer, Jessie."

"A *blond* surfer," Lisa pointed out.

Jessie nodded. "So?"

"So," Lisa said impatiently, "on your list of undesirables, big, blond surfing hunks rank somewhere around an oil slick."

The guy pushed off the pier railing and began to head toward them. Jessie's breath caught in her throat. She saw how all the girls around them checked him out. Guys like him *never* went for her. Maybe he wasn't heading for her after all. Maybe he was coming over to talk to Kelly. Guys like him were always coming over to talk to Kelly. But just then, he caught her eye again, and he smiled. Jessie found herself smiling back.

"Earth to Jessie," Kelly said. "What about Slater?"

"Slater who?" Jessie said.

▲   ▼   ▲

Slater narrowed his eyes. He elbowed Zack.

"Ow!" Zack protested.

"Take a look at what's heading for Kelly, preppy," Slater advised him. "It's hunk-a-mania time."

Zack sighted the walking disaster. Too tall. Too muscular. Too tan. Too perfect. Even his teeth were perfect, Zack noted sourly as the guy flashed a smile. "How do you know he's heading for Kelly?" he asked Slater.

"Because Jessie wouldn't give him the time of day," Slater chortled.

"Wait a second," Zack said. "Take another look.

I think the hunk is after *your* girl."

"Big deal," Slater said confidently. "She'll freeze him out in ten seconds." He watched, a smile on his face, waiting for the guy to self-destruct and slink away. Eight seconds passed. Then fifteen. Thirty.

Wait a second. Was that a *smile* on Jessie's face? A sparkle in her eye? A blush on her cheek? What was going on?

Slater heard the sound of Jessie's ringing laugh. His heart sank down into his sneakers. Was she *encouraging* this dimwit? A guy who belonged in Tanners Anonymous? A guy who thought Life's a Beach should be the United States motto? A guy who spent more time blow-drying his hair than *Jessie* did?

Slater noticed that a ring toss booth was right behind Jessie. If he was lucky, she wouldn't turn around. "C'mon," he said gruffly. "I feel like a game of ring toss."

"Good idea, Slater," Screech said approvingly. "You need a little distraction. Let's go."

▲   ▼   ▲

"Wow," Jessie cooed. "Did you really surf in Hawaii?"

"It was awesome. So what's your name, babe?"

"Uh—"

"Jessie," Kelly supplied.

"Right," Jessie said. "And this is Kelly and Lisa."

"Excellent. I'm Thunder. Really, it's Theodore Thunderbird Thorpe. My mom had me in the backseat of a T-bird. She didn't get to the hospital on time."

"Cool," Jessie said.

"No, it was summer, so it was pretty hot," Thunder said. "It was right at the beach, too. My mom was a surfer's chick."

"So you could say that surfing's in your genes," Jessie said.

"Nah. I never surf in my jeans. I like, wear a wet suit mostly."

"That's not what I . . ." Jessie stopped. What would a *girl* girl say? "Awesome," she finished.

"So do you live around here?" Thunder asked.

Jessie nodded. "How about you?"

"L.A.," Thunder said. "I go to Hollywood Hills High."

Hollywood Hills was the coolest school in Los Angeles, not to mention the richest. The school parking lot looked like a Porsche dealership.

"Cool," Jessie said. She wondered how long she could continue to talk in adjectives. And Hollywood Hills just wasn't her style.

But you're changing your style, Jessie, she told herself sternly. And what better guy to do it with than Thunder Thorpe?

"Man, that guy in the baseball cap is really checking you out," Thunder said, looking over the top of Jessie's head. "I guess you're used to that, though, being such a gorgeous babe and all."

Not really, Jessie almost said. She bit her lip and gave a soft giggle instead. "Well, sure," she said. "Totally."

Lisa and Kelly gave each other incredulous looks. Had Jessie been kidnapped by extraterrestrials and an alien been placed in her body?

Just then, the group that Thunder had been with came up to them. The guys were almost as cute as Thunder. Although the girls were gorgeous, they didn't exactly look welcoming.

"Meet my gang," Thunder said. "We all go to Hollywood Hills High. This is Jason, Shane, Branson, Heather, Tiffany, and Star. Guys, this is Jessie and, uh . . ."

"Kelly and Lisa," Lisa supplied sweetly.

The girl Thunder had called Star slid her glittering green gaze over Kelly and Lisa and rested on Jessie for a long moment before returning to Thunder. "We're out of here," she said.

"It's totally boring," Tiffany complained.

"We thought we'd head for Zorro's," Star said, naming a popular club.

"Excellent." Thunder looked at Jessie. "You guys want to come?"

"Gee, I don't know," Jessie said.

"We know the guy at the door. You'll get in," Thunder assured her.

"Isn't there a big cover charge?" Kelly asked doubtfully. "I don't think I can afford it."

Star's gaze flicked over Kelly. "Gosh, that's too bad," she murmured. "Maybe we should try the Frank Shack."

Kelly felt her cheeks burn. Star's comment had definitely been sarcastic. But no one else seemed to have heard it.

"Anyway, that place is off-limits for me," Jessie said ruefully. "Even if my mom is out of town, I still wouldn't feel right going."

"Then I'll hang out here with you," Thunder said.

Kelly noticed Star's green eyes get suddenly hard, so that they glittered even brighter. But almost as soon as she noticed it, the look was gone and replaced by a warm smile.

"I've got a fabulous idea," Star said. "Let's all go to Jessie's. No parents!"

"Whoa," Branson said. "Par-*ty*."

"Excellent," Shane said.

"I guess," Heather said with a yawn. "It's better than being bored to death here."

Jessie felt her heart pound. She had promised her mother that she'd keep things low-key. The last thing she should do was to invite a gang of strangers over. But then Thunder winked at her, and her heart did a back flip and pulled her conscience underwater. Jessie felt it go down, down, down until it disappeared.

Ignoring the worry in Lisa and Kelly's eyes, Jessie smiled at her new friends. She was going to be a daring girl, a girl who did things on the spur of the moment. Not careful, responsible, *boring* Jessie. She was going to be a risk taker.

"I think it's a great idea," she said. "Let's go!"

Chapter 4

▲ ▼ ▲ ▼ ▲ ▼ ▲

Zack, Slater, and Screech heard Jessie's invitation. Screech choked on his chili dog, Zack let out a smothered yawp, and Slater yelped. The rings they had paid for left their hands involuntarily and flew toward the pegs.

They all turned and stared at Jessie, forgetting that they were incognito. Luckily, she was too busy smiling at Thunder to notice. The two of them led the whole gang to the exit.

"I don't believe this," Slater said. "She invited a whole gang of strangers over!"

"Did you see the guy with the muscles?" Zack said. "The one that was staring at Kelly?"

"I did," Screech said. "He was cute."

"Shut up, Screech," Zack groaned.

"Well, you asked," Screech pointed out.

The vendor spoke behind them. "Yo. Guys!"

Zack, Slater, and Screech didn't hear. They were staring at the space where the loves of their lives had stood just a moment ago, before being whisked away by a trio of guys who looked like they'd be featured on the next episode of "Lives of the Gorgeous, Famous, and Very, Very Rich."

"What are we going to do?" Slater wondered. "We can't let the girls have a huge party without us."

"Somehow I don't think we're invited," Zack said.

"And there's no way we can crash," Slater said mournfully. "They'll spot us right away."

"Yo! You with the caps! The baseball team!"

Zack, Slater, and Screech turned around. The vendor held up the rings that they'd just tossed. "Wake up, fellas. You won." Reaching behind him for the prizes, he handed them three huge, ten-gallon Stetsons.

Zack took his hat and gazed at it, thinking hard. It had a brim the size of a dinner plate.

Slowly, he grinned. "You're right, Slater. Zack, Slater, and Screech can't crash." He put on the hat, which sunk down to his ears, hiding his face. "But Tex, Curly, and the Kid can!"

▲　　　▼　　　▲

When Zack, Slater, and Screech got to the Spano house, the sound of music and laughter traveled over the dark green lawn.

"Wow," Screech said, snapping his fingers to the tune. "It sounds like they're having fun in there."

"They sure are," Slater said grimly. He plopped his hat way down on his head and hooked his fingers through his belt loops. "Ready, Tex?"

"Yup," Zack drawled.

"Git along, little dogies," Screech agreed.

The three of them loped toward the front door. Their ring was answered instantly by Star. She was now barefoot, and she was carrying a bottle of Perrier.

"Howdy, ma'am," Zack said in an exaggerated twang. "I'm Tex Morris, and this here is Curly and the Kid."

"So?" Star said. She eyed them dubiously.

"We're friends of Jessie's," Slater said. He didn't bother to try to fake an accent. He wasn't good at scamming like Zack was. But if Star didn't move out of the doorway soon, he'd forget about using the Morris approach and move straight to the Slater method: muscle.

"Oh," Star said.

"We flew in on Curly's daddy's private jet," Zack said. He wished Star would stand aside and let them in. Any minute now, one of the girls would see them!

"Ohhh," Star said. She gave them a warm smile. "Welcome."

Zack tweaked her cheek as he passed. "You sure are a purty little filly."

Star gave Slater a lush smile. "Make yourself at home, Curly."

"Thank you kindly, ma'am. This here party looks as wild as a prairie dog in a windstorm," Zack said, moving quickly into the hall.

"Don't you think you're overdoing it?" Slater muttered as they took their places in the shadows of the hall to search the packed living room.

"No way, pardner," Zack said. "I'll go check the family room."

Slater frowned as he scanned the living room. The room was crammed with kids, none of whom Slater had ever seen before. Even as he stood there, the doorbell rang again and more kids flowed through the front door. Everyone seemed to know Star, at least. Music was blasting, kids were dancing, and a burly, muscle-bound guy tried to moonwalk and sent a living-room lamp tottering. Slater raced over to save it before it crashed to the floor.

"This is getting out of hand," he said when Zack returned.

"I'll say," Zack remarked as someone knocked over a glass of cola on Mrs. Spano's new pale peach rug. "They're setting up a miniature golf course in the family room. They're using oranges for balls and Mrs. Spano's antique andirons as clubs."

"Where could Jessie be?" Slater asked. "She should put a stop to this."

Screech came up to them, munching on a sandwich. "She's not in the kitchen," he announced. "But somebody is making some great sandwiches. And there's lasagna and fried chicken, too."

"They're cleaning out the refrigerator!" Slater exclaimed worriedly.

Screech shook his head. "No, they're just taking out all the food. I don't think they're wiping up at all. As a matter of fact, someone dropped a jar of chocolate syrup in the vegetable drawer. Of course, I happen to *like* chocolate-covered broccoli, but I realize it's an acquired taste."

Slater let out a groan. This party was definitely turning into an out-of-control situation. Where *was* Jessie?

▲   ▼   ▲

Jessie felt a thrill go through her as Thunder moved closer to her in the hammock. "So tell me, babe," he said, "what do you like to do on weekends?"

Jessie thought frantically. Somehow she didn't think that marching in the Women's Right to Equality Parade would impress Thunder. And studying was definitely out. Not to mention bribing Slater with chocolate-chip cookies so that he'd go with her to a foreign film.

"Go to the beach," she blurted. She couldn't go wrong with that one. Besides, it was true.

"Hey, me, too," Thunder said. "It's awesome how much we have in common."

You, me, and every other teenager in the state of California. "It's rilly awesome," Jessie said.

"This is nice, sitting here," Thunder said as the hammock swung gently. "It's like being on my board."

Actually, it's kind of boring, Jessie thought. So far, all they'd talked about were the waves Thunder had caught last Saturday. But maybe she wasn't giving him a chance. He reached for her hand, and she felt dizzy. That *must* mean she liked him. Or maybe she was just getting queasy from the hammock.

"It would be cool if you could watch me on Saturday," Thunder said. He squeezed her hand. "You'd love it."

If Slater had said something so egotistical, he would have grinned to show her that he was just joking. Jessie looked for signs of a sense of humor in Thunder's light blue eyes. But they only looked sincere. Sincere and . . . dumb.

Not dumb, Jessie. Sweet. Think of him as your very own golden retriever puppy. "I'd love to,"

Jessie said. She pictured herself on the beach, watching her boyfriend surf for hours. It wasn't exactly her idea of a perfect Saturday. But other girls liked it! She could, too. Somewhere there was a girl in North Dakota shoveling her driveway and *dreaming* of a chance to sit on a beach and watch someone like Thunder surf. How could Jessie turn it down?

"You know," Thunder said, "just because I'm totally into surfing doesn't mean I don't have other interests. I wouldn't want you to think I wasn't an all-around type guy. I have, like, higher interests."

Jessie sat up, encouraged. "Oh? What else do you like—reading, plays, art, politics, photography, music?"

"Hang gliding," Thunder said modestly.

▲   ▼   ▲

Zack cruised the family room again, looking for Jessie. On his way back to the living room, he bumped smack into Kelly.

"Weeell, howdy, little lady," he drawled nervously in his down-home accent. He pulled his hat down even farther and started to inch away. "I was just heading to tie on the feed bag, y'all excuse me, heah?"

Kelly giggled. "Hi, Zack."

Sighing, Zack tilted his hat brim up. "How'd you know it was me?"

"That was a terrible accent," Kelly said. "What are you doing here?"

Zack knew that Kelly would be furious if she knew that the guys had tailed them tonight. "I heard the noise, and I figured you girls forgot to invite me," he said, flashing her his most honest-seeming smile.

Kelly gave him a suspicious look. "You can hear us all the way over in your house?"

Zack nodded.

Kelly bit her lip worriedly. "Things *are* getting kind of loud. I was just looking for Jessie. Somebody just barfed on Mrs. Spano's couch."

"I was looking for her, too," Zack said. "I heard two guys talking about making a giant milkshake in the washing machine."

"We've *got* to find her," Kelly said anxiously. "But I've looked everywhere!"

"She's probably with Thunder," Zack said, thinking hard.

"How do you know about Thunder?" Kelly asked him suspiciously.

Zack could have bitten his tongue off. "I heard some guys talking about him," he said.

Kelly lifted an eyebrow.

"I met him when I came in."

Kelly's eyebrow arched even higher.

"I had a psychic vision?" Zack tried.

Kelly backed him against the wall. Normally, he wouldn't have minded. Her perfume floated toward him, and she stood very close. But the icy expression in her eyes wasn't exactly come-hither.

"Spill it, Zack," she rapped out. "Were you following us before?"

Zack nodded. "Just a little bit," he said.

"Just a *little* bit? You mean all the way to the pier and back?"

Zack nodded again.

"Whatever happened to 'I trust Kelly completely'?" Kelly demanded.

"I do!" Zack hastened to assure her. "But I thought a little spying couldn't hurt."

Kelly crossed her arms. "This is just like you, Zack Morris. Not only can't you trust me, you have to sneak around behind my back, invading my privacy. You promised me you were through with scheming."

"I am!" Zack insisted. "This isn't scheming, Kelly. This is . . . uh, scamming."

Kelly didn't say anything. She was really angry, Zack noted nervously. And when Kelly got really angry, he knew that he'd done something really bad.

"I'm sorry, Kelly," he said humbly. "I guess I don't feel secure about us yet. I mean, we just got back together."

"Oh, Zack." Kelly leaned against the wall next to him. "I thought this time was going to be different. I thought we were going to be honest with each other, trust each other. Remember all the promises we made?"

Now Zack really felt terrible. He was the one who had made all the promises. Kelly had always been honest. She'd always trusted him.

Just then, they heard a crash from the kitchen. They exchanged concerned glances.

"We can talk about this later," Kelly said. "It can wait. But if we don't find Jessie soon, Mrs. Spano won't have a house to come home to!"

Chapter 5

▲ ▼ ▲ ▼ ▲ ▼ ▲

On his second sweep of the backyard, Zack finally spotted Jessie and Thunder under the dark trees.

"They're in the hammock," he told Kelly. "Let's go."

Kelly hung back a moment. "Do you think we should?"

A large crash from the house was followed by a war whoop. "It's time to party!" someone yelled.

"C'mon," Kelly said grimly, and they hurried down the lawn toward the hammock.

"Jessie," Kelly called as they approached, "I think you'd better come inside."

"Things are getting out of hand," Zack added.

Jessie sprang off the hammock. She looked almost *relieved*, Kelly noted. Could it be that she wasn't as enthralled with Thunder as she appeared to be?

"What's going on?" she asked.

Zack and Kelly filled her in, and Jessie turned pale. "Oh, my gosh," she said. "My mother will flip out. She'll never let me stay alone again!"

Thunder slid off the hammock. "Whoa. This is a bogus situation. I'm sorry, Jessie. I'll throw everybody out."

The four of them hurried back up the lawn and into the house. When they entered the kitchen, Jessie let out a shriek. Every single food item from the refrigerator seemed to be sitting on the kitchen table. Knives dripping mustard and mayonnaise were strewn around the counters. Soda was spilled on the floor. And someone had tried to make a sculpture out of the ice from the refrigerator's crushed-ice dispenser. They'd abandoned the attempt, and the ice-sculpture was now melting on top of the stove.

"This is awful!" Jessie wailed.

Thunder peeked through the door into the living room. "Who *are* all these people?" he wondered aloud.

Just then, Star walked into the kitchen. A smile was on her face, but it was instantly replaced with a worried expression when she saw everyone. "What's happened in here?" she asked.

"The demolition derby roared through, I guess," Jessie said. "Thunder, you've got to get rid of them."

"Done deal, babe," Thunder said.

Kelly put her arm around Jessie's shoulder. "Don't worry, Jess. We'll help you clean it all up tomorrow."

Zack nodded. "Count me in."

"Me, too," Star said. "I feel sort of responsible."

"It's not your fault," Jessie said. "Come on, Thunder. Let's head 'em up and move 'em out."

"I'll help," Star said quickly.

Everyone started out of the kitchen just as Slater walked in. He gave Jessie a long, steady look.

"Slater, what are you doing here?" Jessie asked nervously.

"Looking for you," Slater said. He glanced at Thunder. "I guess I found you."

"Thunder's going to help me get rid of the crowd," Jessie said.

"Here's one less for you to worry about," Slater said evenly. He walked across the kitchen and straight out the back door into the night.

"Who was that rude dude?" Thunder asked.

Jessie wrung her hands. "My ex-boyfriend," she said.

Kelly and Zack exchanged glances. *Ex*-boyfriend? That would be news to Slater!

▲   ▼   ▲

Slater paused on the dark back porch just long enough to hear Jessie say that he was her ex. He strode quickly off the porch, his face burning, and then stopped under the shadows of the huge oak in Jessie's backyard. He had to stop; he couldn't breathe. He felt like someone had been tap dancing on his heart.

Ex-boyfriend! He thought they were just going to cool it. Every once in a while, he and Jessie got in a fight and told each other they were going to date other people. Each of them kept their Saturday nights free and usually ended up watching TV alone. The only time they even *looked* at anybody else was when the other one was around, just for the jealousy factor. After a couple of weeks, they ended up missing each other too much, and one of them always made the first move to make up.

But this time, Jessie really meant it!

A shadow emerged from the dark back porch and drifted toward him. Slater turned to go. He wasn't in the mood to face anybody right now.

"Hey, hold on." The figure moved closer, and Slater saw that it was Star. Her chestnut hair waved around her face, and her light green eyes gleamed. Slater realized slowly that she was a definite dish. He'd been so wrapped up in Jessie he hadn't even noticed. That sure wasn't like him.

Star looked up at him with an intent gaze. "Tell me if it's none of my business," she said. "But you didn't look too happy in there."

"It's none of your business," Slater said flatly.

"So you and Jessie used to go out?" Star asked.

Slater winced; it hurt him to think of him and Jessie in the past tense. "Yeah," he said shortly. "So what?"

"So you're hurting," Star said simply.

Slater turned away. "I gotta go."

But a small, soft hand on his bare arm stopped him. "Maybe I could see it because I know what it's like," Star said. "That's all I wanted to say."

Her hand slowly slipped off his arm, and she started to walk away.

"Wait," Slater said, and she stopped and turned around. Why shouldn't he accept comfort if someone offered it? Even if that someone just happened to be a knockout? "Want to clear out of here and get some coffee or something?" he asked.

The moon slid from behind a cloud and lit Star with a silvery light. She seemed to gleam as a smile slowly lit up her face. "I'd like that very much," she said quietly.

▲　　▼　　▲

Star was easy to be with. He didn't have to talk much. They decided on iced teas to go and sat on the beach, talking about nothing. It was a calm end to such a tumultuous night. Star was pretty cool,

Slater decided. It was refreshing to be with a girl who knew when to shut up.

And she was so small and delicate. Jessie was tall and strong and met him eye to eye. She strode through life with a lifted chin, needing no help from anybody. Star melted against him, needing his arm to traverse the soft sand. Slater liked it. He liked feeling needed.

It was late when Slater got home. He eased open the squeaky front door carefully. His parents weren't really strict, but he was definitely past his curfew.

The house was dark and silent, so his parents must be asleep. Slater slipped out of his sneakers, anyway, and tiptoed across the living room. He jumped when he saw a dark form in the big easy chair by the window.

"Dad!" Slater exclaimed. "You scared me!"

"Sorry, A. C.," his dad said. "I didn't hear you come in."

Slater paused. What was his father doing sitting in the dark, staring out the window? A pack of cigarettes was sitting on the small table at his side. He'd quit smoking ten years ago!

"Are you smoking, Dad?" he asked.

His father grimaced and tossed the cigarette he was holding onto the table. "Not really. I haven't lit one. I've just been holding it."

"Oh," Slater said. "Is everything okay?" he asked tentatively.

His father looked at him for a long moment. "Everything's just fine," he said finally. "Just fine," he repeated. "Go ahead up to bed, son."

As Slater headed upstairs to his room, he tried to tell himself that everything *was* fine. But he had a feeling that for the first time in his life, his father had lied to him.

Amazingly enough, Slater fell asleep as soon as his head hit the pillow. When he opened his eyes, the sun was shining and a breeze lifted the curtains at his window. Another beautiful day in Palisades, Slater thought, groggily raising himself on his elbows. A perfect day for the beach, or tennis, or a pickup basketball game. But he knew he wasn't going to do any of those things. He was going to put on an apron and clean Jessie's house.

Even though he didn't want to see her, he had been her friend before he was her boyfriend. And Jessie needed all the friends she could get today. The Spano house had been trashed, and Jessie would be grounded until college if they didn't put it right.

Slater pulled on his jeans and an old T-shirt and went into the kitchen. There was a note on the refrigerator saying his parents were out doing errands. Good. He couldn't take any more family trauma today.

He grabbed a quick breakfast and decided to jog over to Jessie's house. The air was still cool enough. As he ran, he thought over last night again. Maybe he had been too quick to decide that it was over with Jessie for good. Maybe they both had needed to let off steam. Even *girls* needed to let off steam once in a while, Slater told himself. Jessie couldn't be seriously interested in that Thunder person.

When he got to the Spano house, Zack and Kelly were already there. With a rueful grin, Kelly handed him a broom.

"There's some broken glass in the powder room," she told him. "Lisa and Screech are on their way over."

Jessie came into the room. Her hair was tied back in a ponytail, and a streak of dirt was smeared on her white T-shirt. Her face lit up when she saw Slater. "Hi," she said. "I didn't think you'd—"

"Didn't think I'd what?" he asked her.

"Didn't think you'd come," Jessie said falteringly.

Slater bit back a quick reply. He could see that Jessie really was pleased to see him. "Of course I came," he said gruffly. "This place needs all the help it can get."

"Thank you," Jessie said softly.

"How's the washing machine coming?" Kelly asked. She was spraying a can of stain remover on the rug.

Jessie grimaced. "It's really hard to clean out. There's still milk and a couple of eggs in there. And my back is killing me from reaching in to get all that gunk out."

"Why don't you just run the machine through a wash cycle?" Slater suggested. "The filter will catch the eggshells. Let the machine do the work."

Jessie laughed. "Slater, that's brilliant!"

"Wait a second," Zack said, pausing with a wad of paper towels in his hand. "Did I just hear the words *Slater* and *brilliant* in the same sentence?"

Kelly giggled. "And was that Jessie saying them?"

Jessie threw a dustrag at them and laughed. "If you guys don't stop, I won't spring for the pizzas at lunch."

"Did someone say pizza?" Screech said, poking his head in the door.

"Now I'm *really* glad I came," Lisa added, coming in. She was wearing a pair of baggy coveralls, and everyone gaped at her. They'd never seen her in anything less than a perfectly coordinated outfit.

"This is too much to take," Zack said. "First Jessie says Slater is brilliant, then Lisa shows up in coveralls." He leaned over to Kelly. "Feel my forehead. I think I'm delirious."

"I didn't say Slater was brilliant," Jessie said with a grin. "I said his *idea* was."

Lisa giggled. "And watch this, Zack." She pulled open the snaps on her coveralls to reveal a perfectly ironed yellow playsuit. Then, out of one of the huge pockets, she pulled out a pair of matching sandals. The other pocket held a makeup kit and comb.

"I have the mirror," Screech said, reaching into his overalls and taking out a makeup mirror.

"Since you're not delirious, I guess you can finish cleaning the family room, Zack," Jessie said wickedly.

Kelly peered out the window. "I wonder where Star is. She said she'd be over first thing in the morning."

"She called," Jessie informed them. "She got grounded by her father. She missed her curfew last night."

That's funny, Slater thought. *I dropped her off at her house at eleven o'clock. Maybe her father is really strict.*

"That's too bad," Kelly murmured.

Zack shot Kelly a curious look. It looked as though she didn't buy Star's excuse. And it wasn't like Kelly not to trust someone's word. He'd have to get the dirt on this later, though. Now he had some more pressing dirt to tackle. Namely, the stuff ground into the family-room rug!

▲   ▼   ▲

With the whole gang pitching in, the mess was cleaned up in no time. By one o'clock, Jessie's house was sparkling again.

Jessie leaned on a broom and surveyed the kitchen. "It looks perfect, guys," she said. "There's only one problem."

"Oh, no," Zack groaned. "Don't tell me we forgot to clean something. I think I've rubbed off all the skin on my palms from scrubbing."

"No," Jessie said. "It's just that my mom is going to *know* something went on here. This place has *never* been this clean."

Everyone laughed. Kelly finished throwing the remains of their quick pizza lunch into a garbage bag, and then tied it off.

"I'm going to head home for a shower," she said. "Maybe we can all meet up at the Max later."

"Sounds cool," Slater said. He slid along the counter so he'd be closer to Jessie. When Lisa and Kelly started toward the door and Zack and Screech started a conversation, he had his chance.

"Why don't we cool off in the ocean?" he suggested to Jessie. "I can run home and get my car. Or we could take your mom's."

Jessie looked uneasy. "That sounds nice, Slater," she said hesitantly.

Slater jumped off the counter. "So let's go." He felt relief course through him. Despite all the hard work this morning, the question of his parents' troubles was never far from his mind. He couldn't forget seeing his father sitting there all alone in the dark. He had to talk to someone about it or he'd bust. And Jessie was the only one who could make him feel okay.

"But I can't," Jessie blurted. "I told Star I'd meet

her at the beach where the Hollywood Hills crowd hangs out."

"I thought she was grounded."

"She thought her father would give in by this afternoon," Jessie said faintly. Why was Slater looking at her that way, as if she'd just shot his dog? "If she plays music real loud and drives him crazy, he lets her go out. So . . ."

"No problem," Slater said, his face tight.

Jessie hesitated. Something in Slater's face told her that this was important to him. Something was wrong, and it wasn't just the coolness between them. "Come with me," she urged.

"Thanks, anyway," Slater said. "I don't want to horn in on you and your new friends Star and Rain Cloud."

"Thunder," Jessie said, annoyed.

"Whatever. See you." Slater stalked out of the kitchen, leaving Jessie with a clean house and an uneasy heart.

Chapter 6

▲ ▼ ▲ ▼ ▲ ▼ ▲

On Monday morning, Zack waited by Kelly's locker until the bell, but she didn't show up. He was worried as he headed for his first class. He and Kelly hadn't been alone all weekend. Saturday night they'd gone to the movies with Slater to cheer him up, since Jessie had had a date with Thunder. And Sunday Kelly had gone on a picnic with her family.

Zack couldn't stop thinking about Friday night, when Kelly had looked at him with accusing eyes and said *I thought this time we were going to be honest with each other, trust each other.*

Zack groaned aloud. There was nobody as good as Kelly when it came to making a guy feel guilty about being a jerk.

"Mr. Morris," Mr. Dickerson said icily, "I realize that American history does not inspire the delight that video games do for your generation, but I *do* think you could manage to restrain yourself in class."

Zack sat up. "Sorry, Mr. Dickerson."

"Now, back to nineteen twelve," Mr. Dickerson said. "Zack, why don't you remind the class what I was speaking about."

Zack searched his brain and came up blank. His notebook was open, but it was blank, too. All he'd been thinking about was Kelly. "Nineteen twelve, sir," he said helpfully.

Mr. Dickerson tapped his pencil on his desk irritably. "The *Titanic*, Mr. Morris," he said. "The great ship that went down to the bottom of the sea. Which, incidentally, is where your grade is headed if you don't start paying attention."

The class snickered, and Zack gave Mr. Morris a weak smile and picked up his pen. He had to concentrate. He'd see Kelly in science class third period, at least. He could put off worrying until then.

He spent second period dozing in study hall, and when the bell rang, he shot to his feet. He hurried out of study hall and sprang for the stairs. He couldn't wait to see Kelly.

And there she was, coming down the hall toward him, smiling. And the smile was for him. *Whew*, Zack thought. She couldn't be too disappointed in him, then.

"Hi," he said. "I waited by your locker this morning."

"I had to see a teacher," Kelly said.

"Good," Zack said in relief. "I thought you still might be mad at me about the other night."

"I am," Kelly said pleasantly.

Zack did a double take. "You are?"

"Absolutely," Kelly said, taking him by the arm and steering him to a less busy corner of the hall. "I don't want to have a boyfriend who doesn't trust me."

"Kelly, I do trust—" Zack started, but Kelly put her hand on his mouth.

"Zack, you can tell me until you're blue in the face, but it won't mean anything except that you're out of breath," she said. "Actions speak louder than words."

"Mmmmfffphffff," Zack said.

"What?" Kelly asked.

Zack gently removed Kelly's hand from his mouth. "I said I agree. That's why I'm going to prove to you that I do trust you."

"Great," Kelly said. "And I know just how you can do it."

Suddenly, Zack decided he wasn't crazy about where this conversation was heading. "What do you mean?" he asked cautiously.

"I have an idea for your science project," Kelly said. "You're going to collaborate with me."

Zack relaxed. This was definitely okay. The more time he spent with Kelly, the better he liked it. "Great," he said. "But I have to warn you, the aquarium idea is out."

"I already thought of what we can do," Kelly said. "And I cleared it with Mrs. Galluchio."

"Okay," Zack said cautiously, beginning to be suspicious again. "What's your idea?"

"An experiment in trust," Kelly said. "Here's the deal. You're going to have to completely rely on me."

"That's easy," Zack said, fixing her with his most seductive gaze. "I already rely on you, Kelly."

"But this time you're going to be blindfolded," Kelly said. "And I'm going to lead you around. I'm going to feed you, bring you to your classes—every-where—for a week."

"*Everywhere*?" Zack asked.

"Well, almost everywhere," Kelly amended.

"This sounds like the easiest *A* I'll ever get," Zack said.

"We'll see," Kelly said.

"But I'm not crazy about being the subject here," Zack said. "Can't we blindfold someone else? Like Screech?"

Kelly shook her head. "Take it or leave it. Think of yourself as a lab rat."

"Gee, thanks."

Kelly giggled, and the bell rang. "C'mon," she said. "We can talk about this later over lunch. It's spaghetti day."

"Don't worry about me," Zack groaned. "I'll just nibble on some cheese."

▲   ▼   ▲

The next day, Kelly came in with a silk scarf that she tied around Zack's eyes. It felt soft and cool against his skin, but he couldn't see a thing.

"Too tight?" Kelly asked. "Are you okay?"

"Sure," Zack said. "I feel fine." As fine as he *could* feel plunged into total blackness with the noise of footsteps pounding behind him and in front of him. Voices swirled and eddied around him, and Zack already felt dizzy.

"I'll lead you to Mr. Dickerson's class," Kelly explained, taking his arm. "Once you're in your seat, you can take off the blindfold. When the bell rings, put it on again and wait for me to lead you to your next class."

"Check," Zack said. Kelly began to walk, and he heard footsteps coming toward them. He flinched.

"I've got you, Zack. Trust me."

He shuffled forward, trying to remember how long the hallway was. There was a turn in about fifty paces, he judged. They kept on walking while students chattered and laughed around them. Someone bumped into him from behind.

"Sorry," a voice said, and faded.

They must be almost at the turn, and Kelly was

still going straight. She was going to lead him right into the brick wall!

"Kelly, pay attention," Zack said. "There's a wall up ahead. You wouldn't want to smash these perfect cheekbones, would you?" He tried to joke, but his voice sounded a little shaky.

"Trust me, Zack." Kelly's voice was calm, and they continued on doggedly. Zack's footsteps began to drag. The wall was just ahead, he knew it. Was Kelly trying to teach him a lesson by running him straight into it?

"Zack, come on. You'll be late for class."

Dizzy, Zack tried to walk faster. But if he walked faster, he'd smash into the wall!

He couldn't stand it anymore. Zack reached up and tore off the blindfold. The wall was a good twenty paces away.

He looked over at Kelly. She smirked at him. "A real easy *A*, huh?" she said.

With a deep sigh, Zack handed the blindfold back to Kelly so that she could tie it on again.

"It's okay, Kelly," he said. "If this is what it takes to keep you, I'll do it. You can even gag me if you want."

"Don't tempt me," Kelly said.

▲   ▼   ▲

On Wednesday afternoon, the next phase of Kelly's experiment was to take place at the mall. Lisa needed to give Jessie her first shopping lesson, so the rest of the gang tagged along, too.

"Don't peek, Zack," Kelly warned as they approached the escalator. "I'll tell you when to get on."

"Can't we take the stairs?" Zack asked. "After that car ride, I feel kind of sick. I don't want to get on another moving vehicle."

"Don't be silly. One, two, three," Kelly said, and Zack stepped smoothly onto the escalator.

Slater stepped onto it with Screech. Jessie was just ahead. If he moved closer, he would get a faceful of silky light brown curls.

Lisa was giving Jessie pointers on the most efficient way to shop.

"First of all, always carry a little calculator," she said. "That's the only way to figure out percentages on sale items. Once, I was standing there trying to figure out what thirty percent off fifty-two dollars was and a woman snatched the silk blouse I wanted right off the rack!" Lisa shuddered. "It taught me a lesson."

"I'll bet," Jessie said. She had never been very interested in clothes. Her wardrobe consisted of jeans, T-shirts, and an occasional pretty sweater.

"I think we'll start with skirts today," Lisa said. "Accessories will take a full day, so we can do that on Saturday."

"I'm going to the beach on Saturday," Jessie said.

Lisa gave her a frustrated look. "Are you serious about this or not?" she complained.

The escalator drew toward the top. "Ready?" Kelly asked Zack, her hand on his arm.

"Ready," Zack said. "Do you think we can sit by the fountain for a while when we get to the top? I feel carsick. Or escalator sick, I can't tell."

"Now!" Kelly said, but Zack wasn't listening, and he tripped and started to fall. Kelly kept him upright, but right behind him, Lisa tripped over his feet. She was wearing brand-new shoes and began to slide along the slick floor, dragging Jessie with her. Slater reached over to help, but his arm got caught in Jessie's purse strap. He toppled, bringing Screech down with him, who flailed his arms and hit Kelly, who lost her balance. Kelly, Lisa, Jessie, Slater, and Screech all ended up on the floor. The only one left standing was Zack.

"Come on, guys," he said, turning his head this way and that. "No fooling around. Where did you go?"

They all laughed, holding onto each other. Slater found his arm around Jessie. Their eyes met, and they stopped laughing.

Jessie stood up, dusting off her skirt. "We should get started, Lisa."

"Let me make a quick reconnaissance run first,"

Lisa said. "It's crucial. Then I'll decide what order to hit the stores in."

"Okay," Jessie said. It wasn't okay. She didn't want to be left with Slater. Kelly was already leading Zack away, and Screech had drifted over to look at turtles in the pet shop.

Well, now was as good a time as any to begin the next phase of their relationship: pure, platonic friendship. Jessie turned to him.

"I hear you're seeing Star," she said.

Slater nodded. "We had a date the other night, yeah."

"She's really nice," Jessie said. "I'm really having fun with her and her friends."

"I'm glad," Slater said. "I notice you've been dressing differently. What happened to your jeans and T-shirts?"

"I just thought it was time for a new look," Jessie said, smoothing the skirt she'd shortened.

"It's not you, Jess," Slater said quietly. "You're trying to dress like Star, and it's just not you."

"How do *you* know? You don't know everything about me!" Jessie cried. Slater didn't think she could be as sexy as Star!

"One thing I *don't* know is how you can stand dating Typhoon."

"Thunder," Jessie snapped. "When are you going to get his name right?"

"When he starts being a normal person with a

normal name," Slater shot back. "His name is Theodore. Ted is acceptable. Theo would be fine. I'd even take Teddy. But Thunder? Give me a break. He sounds like a weatherman."

Jessie tossed her curls. "And what about *Star*? Who does she sound like, a Nobel Prize winner?"

"It makes more sense than Thunder. What's next, Cyclone? Hurricane? Stationary Front?" Slater snarled.

Jessie opened her mouth to shoot back a reply, but Screech had returned and was listening to them. He was carrying a turtle, and he was beaming.

"I'm glad to see you're all taking such an interest in science lately," he said, nodding in approval. "First Kelly and Zack get all fired up about this science project, and now you two are becoming interested in meteorology!"

Lisa came up to them. "Come on, Jessie, we've got some serious shopping to do. If you're going to the beach on Saturday, you'll need a new suit."

"Right." Jessie watched as Slater turned away in disgust. *Who cares?* she thought angrily. If Slater thought he knew her so well, he'd better watch out. She was aiming for a whole new Jessie!

Chapter 7

▲ ▼ ▲ ▼ ▲ ▼ ▲

That night, Slater showered and changed into his jeans and a fresh shirt. He grabbed his car keys and bounded downstairs. His mom was in the kitchen, but instead of fixing dinner, she was sitting at the kitchen table, staring into space.

"Mom, are you okay?" Slater asked, concerned.

She smiled. "I'm fine. Just a little tired. I'm about to start dinner. Where are you off to?"

"I have a date," Slater said. "Didn't you see my note?" He pointed to the refrigerator.

"Oh. No, I missed it. Your father isn't going to be home for dinner, either. He's working late."

Slater instantly felt guilty. "I'm sorry, Mom. Do you want me to cancel my date?"

"Don't be silly," his mother said warmly. "Are you seeing Jessie?"

"Nope." Slater opened the refrigerator and took out the orange juice. He took a swig from the carton, expecting an admonishing look from his mother. But she didn't seem to notice. That made him feel *really* depressed.

"It's with Star," Slater said, replacing the orange juice. "We're going to grab some food and go see a new film that her dad had these special preview tickets for."

"Sounds like fun," his mother said. "Do you like this girl?"

"I guess," Slater said. "I don't know her real well." *And I really miss Jessie.*

"Well, have a good time." His mother started out of the kitchen.

"Aren't you going to fix your dinner?" Slater asked, puzzled.

"I'm going to lie down for a few minutes first. 'Bye, honey."

Slater watched his mother leave the kitchen. She seemed really sad. Cold dread settled to the pit of his stomach. Something was wrong—he could feel it.

Star had asked him to pick her up downtown, where she was having her hair cut. Slater waited outside, drumming on the steering wheel and thinking about his parents.

Star emerged from the salon and waved at him. The setting sun picked out the reddish glints in her hair. She slid into the front seat and smiled. "I hope you haven't been waiting long."

"Not really," Slater answered.

Star's smile faltered. "Well?"

"Oh. Right." Slater turned on the engine. "Hamburgers or pizza?"

"I meant, well, how do I look?" Star asked. "I just spent two and a half hours in there."

"Oh," Slater said. "You look gorgeous." Usually he had no trouble complimenting girls. But usually they didn't *ask* for it.

"Gee, thanks." Star tilted the rearview mirror to study her reflection. "Do you like my highlights?"

"The red? Oh. Sure. Cool."

Star gave him a sidelong look. "Watch it, Slater. All this flattery might go to my head."

Slater laughed. "I'm sorry. To tell you the truth, I've got a bunch of stuff on my mind. Things are kind of weird at home."

Star settled back against the seat with a groan. "Tell me about it. You know the Addams Family? They're, like, *normal* compared to my home situation."

"Really?" Slater asked.

"I call my stepmother Morticia. I swear she's embalmed. She *says* she's twenty-nine, but I swear she's at least forty. And the worst part is my dad practically *faints* when she enters a room. He's completely gone. They just got married last year. It can't last. I give them another six months, tops."

"What about your mom?"

"Who?" Star waved a newly manicured hand. "She lives in Italy. She calls once in a while and talks to me in Italian. I can't even *speak* Italian. On my annual visit, I see her for about five minutes. So you can't tell me about trouble at home, pal. I've been around that block about fifty times."

"Wow," Slater said. "I guess I'm pretty lucky. This is the first time my parents have had problems."

Star twisted in her seat to face him. "What's wrong? Are they fighting?"

"I'm not sure," Slater admitted. "But I've heard these really intense conversations going on. My dad's real quiet and worried looking. And when my mom isn't silent and dragging around, she's practically bursting into tears."

"Oooo, the worst," Star said sagely. "They're trying to put up a good front for you. But something's definitely going on, right?"

"I just wish they'd *tell* me," Slater said in frustration. "This is worse than anything."

Star nodded. "I know. I was twelve when my parents split. For, like, *months* they obviously hated each other. But they had these big, phony smiles on their faces around me. It was disgusting."

"I hear you," Slater said gloomily. He looked over at Star. "Listen," he said suddenly. "Do you want to skip the movie and just talk? We could get some takeout burgers and just head for the beach."

"But these are preview tickets for *Alien Invasion*," Star said. "I'd be like the first person at school to see it."

"Oh. Well, in that case," Slater said, shrugging. He started the engine, but he was stopped when Star slid over on the seat and put her hand on his arm.

"But I'd really rather go to the beach with you," she said softly. "I *do* want to talk."

Slater smiled. For the first time that night, for the first time maybe in *days*, he felt pretty good. Star was a special girl. Maybe he could get over Jessie after all.

▲   ▼   ▲

The next day after school, Kelly cornered Jessie in the hall. She crossed her arms and barricaded Jessie's locker so that Jessie couldn't get to it.

"Have something on your mind, Kelly?" Jessie teased.

"You," Kelly said. "I haven't seen you all week long. And you haven't called me once."

"I've been kind of busy," Jessie said. "Lisa has been giving me shopping lessons. And I've been seeing Thunder, too. But you're right. We should spend more time together. We should schedule that cheerleading lesson. And I want you to teach me how to giggle."

"Jessie, can't we just *talk*?" Kelly pleaded. "Why don't we go to the beach this afternoon? We haven't done that together in so long."

"Don't you have to lead Zack around?" Jessie asked.

Kelly grinned. "I gave him the afternoon off."

"I don't know," Jessie said doubtfully. "I was going to go to the bookstore and get a book on how to flirt."

Kelly sighed. "Oh, Jessie. You don't have to read a book to learn how to flirt. It's simple."

Jessie drew closer. "It is? Tell me."

Kelly looked at her craftily. "If you come to the beach with me, I will."

Jessie nodded. "Okay. But let's take my car."

"Great," Kelly said. "I'll grab my suit and towel from my trunk and meet you in the parking lot."

It felt like old times, Kelly thought as she and Jessie headed for Ocean Boulevard. The breeze lifted their hair and they laughed and talked about the goings-on at Bayside. Jessie didn't mention the Hollywood Hills High crowd once.

They passed the turnoff to Palisades Beach, and Kelly turned to Jessie. "Jess? You missed the turn back there."

"No, I didn't," Jessie said. "I'm going to a different beach. It's just a little farther."

"The beach where Star and Thunder hang out?" Kelly asked.

Jessie nodded. "It's much prettier. You'll love it."

But when they got there, it didn't seem any prettier to Kelly. It seemed like a waste of twenty minutes of sun to her. But she didn't want to spoil the afternoon, so Kelly silently shook out the blanket and got out suntan cream from her tote bag.

Jessie scanned the beach. "Nobody's here," she said.

"What are you talking about?" Kelly said, looking around at the crowd. "The beach is packed." But she knew what Jessie meant. *Star* wasn't there. Or *Thunder*.

Jessie spread some sunblock on her shoulders and turned to Kelly. "So. Tell me. What's the secret of flirting? I can try it on Thunder this weekend." She frowned. "Even though he hasn't asked me out yet."

"I just meant the only secret was to really like the guy," Kelly said. "When you really care about someone, flirting is natural. Your eyes light up, and you smile, and you're interested in what he says. That's all flirting is."

"Oh," Jessie said, sounding disappointed. "I thought you'd have an actual *plan*. Like an outline. A. Establish eye contact. B. Touch him occasionally when you talk. Subdivision 1. Find out his favorite cologne. *You* know."

Kelly laughed. "It's not a term paper, Jessie."

Jessie laughed reluctantly. "I know. But, boy, sometimes I wish it was! Then I might be good at it."

Kelly dug her hand in the warm sand and let it trickle through her fingers. "What about Thunder, Jessie?" she asked in an offhand tone. "Do you really care about him?"

"Sure," Jessie said promptly. "He's really good-looking, isn't he? And he really likes me."

"That's not what I asked," Kelly said.

Jessie shaded her eyes and looked out at the ocean. "I'm having fun, Kelly," she said quietly. "I know that doesn't seem like such a big deal to you, but it is to me. It's *easy* being with Thunder. He doesn't expect things. He doesn't challenge me."

"And you like that?" Kelly asked doubtfully. "That doesn't sound like you."

"Well, it is," Jessie said doggedly. Just then, her face lit up, and she waved. "It's Star," she said.

"Great," Kelly said faintly.

Star came over to them, looking fabulous in a mint green bikini. She knelt down in the sand in front of them. "Jessie! I didn't expect to see you here today! This is fantastic!"

"We just decided to head up this way," Jessie said. "You remember Kelly, right?"

"Sure," Star said. "Listen, I'm really glad I ran into you, Jessie. I was going to call you tonight. I have the most fabulous news. My dad is throwing this huge party Saturday night, and he said I could invite whoever I want! There's going to be all these stars there, and famous producers and directors. Can you come?''

"*Can* I!'' Jessie said, her eyes sparkling. "In a New York minute!''

"Fabulous!'' Star looked at Kelly. "I wish I could invite you, too, Kelly, but my dad said to keep my list super small.''

"It's okay,'' Kelly said. She wouldn't be caught dead at Star's party, she decided. No matter if the biggest stars in Hollywood were there. She was really starting to dislike the girl.

"Oh, no!'' Jessie's face suddenly fell. "I can't go!''

"Why not?'' Star asked. "Is it because of Slater? I don't have to invite him. I know you guys were close.''

"It's not Slater,'' Jessie said.

Star giggled. "Though why you'd want to break up with someone whose daddy is a Texas oil millionaire, I don't know.''

Jessie and Kelly laughed. "Slater's dad was in the army,'' Jessie said. "He's not a millionaire.''

"But at the party he said—''

"That was probably Zack's idea,'' Kelly said. "They were just trying to crash the party in disguise. Slater's just a regular guy.''

"Oh,'' Star said. "So, Jessie, why can't you come to my party then?''

"I'm grounded this weekend," Jessie said. "My mom found out about the party last weekend. Somebody short-sheeted her bed. There's no way she'd let me go to a big party."

"Wow," Star said wistfully. "I wish my father *cared* enough to ground me."

"I thought he grounded you last Saturday," Kelly said. "When you couldn't help us clean up, remember?"

Star shot her an evil look. "Right," she said quickly. "But it was my stepmother who grounded me. He just went along with it." She turned back to Jessie. "You just have to come! Thunder's counting on it. He wants you to be his date."

"Oh, no!" Jessie wailed. "This is just awful."

Star snapped her fingers. "I have a great idea. Why don't you tell your mother you're sleeping at Kelly's house that night? She'll let you do that, right? Then Kelly can cover for you and you can come to the party."

"I don't know . . . ," Jessie said.

"Oh, come on," Star urged. "Why not? I thought you wanted to be a *risk taker*."

Jessie looked at Kelly, and Kelly felt her cheeks flush. She never lied to her parents. Ever. They trusted her, and she wanted to live up to that trust.

"It's okay, Kelly," Jessie said. "You don't have to."

Star gave a negligent shrug. "Sure, Kelly. You

don't have to. I mean, I'd do it for Jessie if I could. I'd do *anything* for a friend. That's what friends are for, right?''

No, Kelly wanted to say. *Friends are for talking you out of doing stupid things, not into them.* But she couldn't.

Kelly felt trapped and frustrated. Star was saying that she was a better friend to Jessie than Kelly was! And Jessie looked so disappointed and upset. What else could she do?

"Okay, Jess," she said quietly. "I'll do it."

Chapter 8

▲ ▼ ▲ ▼ ▲ ▼ ▲

When Slater got home from wrestling practice that day, he bumped into his mom and dad in the doorway of his house. They were just heading out.

"We have an appointment," his father explained, "but we'll be back before dinner. We'll bring home some take-out."

His mother put a hand on his arm. "You'll be home for dinner, won't you?"

Slater nodded. "But I have a date with Star afterward."

His father frowned. "We wanted to have a talk with you this evening, A. C. We have something important to discuss."

This is it, Slater thought with a sense of dread. *This is finally when they tell me they're getting a divorce.* But he might as well get it over with. "I can stick around for a while," Slater said. "I'll call Star and tell her."

"Good," his father said. "Come on, Loretta, we'll be late."

Slater watched them go, a deep frown on his face. Maybe they were heading for their lawyer. Was this the last time he'd see them driving off together? Was this the last time his dad would sleep in the same house?

Sighing, he went inside to call Star. She had her own private number, and she answered on the first ring.

"Hey," he said. "It's Slater. How's it going?"

"Great," Star said. "I just came from catching some rays at the beach."

"Listen, I'm going to be a little late picking you up tonight," Slater said.

"Oh."

"My dad wants to have an important talk tonight. It shouldn't take too long, though," Slater said. "I mean, how many ways can they tell me that they're splitting up?"

"You'd be surprised. They're going to spend, like, an hour telling you how they both love you and this won't make a difference in your life. And how it has nothing to do with you and it's something that just happens. It's a total bore." Star hesitated. "Listen, you can cancel tonight. I mean, if you'd rather be by yourself. I wouldn't be mad. It might be better for you, actually."

"Thanks, Star, that's really sweet," Slater said. "But I think I'll really need someone to talk to."

"Well, okay. If you're sure. . . ."

"I'm sure." Star was so considerate, Slater thought. She knew that sometimes a guy wanted to be alone. But she was there for him when he needed her, too. "I'll see you later," Slater said.

"Okay," Star said. "Listen, maybe it isn't divorce after all."

"Maybe not," Slater said. But Star's words sounded hollow, and he knew she was just trying to make him feel better. Worst of all, in his own heart, he knew she was wrong.

▲   ▼   ▲

Zack saw Kelly and Jessie enter the Max just as he was about to bite into his cheeseburger. He stopped and put it down as Jessie stopped at another table to chat and Kelly headed toward him.

"No!" he cried, crossing two fingers and holding them out to Kelly to ward her off. "You gave me the afternoon off! I can't eat a cheeseburger with a blindfold again."

Kelly grinned as she slid into the booth opposite him. "I thought you did pretty well yesterday," she teased.

"Oh, right," Zack said. "I could have licked the catsup and mustard off my shirt."

Kelly laughed. "Did you?"

"Of course not," Zack said, insulted. "I gave it to Screech. *He* licked it off."

"Don't worry, Zack," Kelly said. "You don't have to wear the blindfold. But you have to admit my experiment is working."

"I'll say," Zack said. "I have complete faith in you now, Kelly. You haven't run me into a wall, tripped me, or thrown me down a flight of stairs." He beamed at her. "I know I can trust you now."

Zack reached across the table and took Kelly's hand. With all this blindfolding, romantic action had certainly decreased this week. Once, he'd tried to put his arm around her and poked her in the eye.

"I've got a great idea," he said. "Tonight, let's go out, just us. There's going to be a full moon. We'll drive down the coast to that little café we found that day—"

Kelly sighed. "Oh, Zack. I can't. I'm too worried about Jessie."

Zack squeezed her hand. "We can talk about it at the café," he said. "Or later. At the beach. Just you and me. Under the full moon. Alone."

Kelly shook her head. "I just couldn't relax."

"I could *help* you relax," Zack said. "Tonight. On the beach. Just you and me. Under a full moon. Alone."

But Kelly didn't even seem to hear him. She

pulled her hand away and frowned. "I think she's getting in over her head," she said worriedly.

Zack sighed and picked up a french fry. As long as Kelly was distracted, he might as well use his hands for eating. "Tell me about it," he said.

As he munched, Kelly filled him in on Star's invitation and how she'd felt trapped into covering for Jessie. Zack put down his cheeseburger and frowned.

"I see what you mean," he said. "It's not like Jessie to ask you to lie for her. She's really under this girl's influence."

"That's it, Zack," Kelly said. "I can sort of see why, too. Star is so pretty and sweet—at least to Jessie. She's always calling her and asking her to do things and listening to her troubles. But I just don't buy it. I don't like how she froze me out the other night when she knew I didn't have any money. And today at the beach, she practically ignored me unless Jessie brought me into the conversation. That's kind of mean."

Zack rolled his eyes. *Kind of mean* was putting it mildly, he thought.

"You know, I shouldn't say this, but . . . " Kelly bit her lip and fiddled with a straw.

"Go ahead, Kelly," Zack said. "I'm sure whatever it is, someone else would have said it a long time ago."

"Well, I could be wrong," Kelly said. "But,

Shane, that guy in Star's crowd—he told me that Star and Thunder were a pretty hot item just a few weeks ago. I think Star is being so nice to Jessie just to be around her and Thunder."

Zack nodded. "Like a spy in the enemy's camp," he said.

"Exactly." Kelly sighed. "And Jessie just doesn't see it. I don't think that Star is a very nice person," Kelly finished.

When Kelly said *that*, it meant that somebody was practically an ax murderer, Zack knew. "Do you want me to talk to Jessie?" he asked.

"Oh, Zack, that would be great," Kelly said. "She'd really listen to you. She just thinks I'm jealous of Star."

Zack and Jessie had been best friends since he'd moved in next door when he was four years old. They'd made mud pies together and played hide-and-seek in each other's backyards. They'd consoled each other and been there for each other countless times. He couldn't let her down now. They always depended on each other to tell each other the truth, even when no one else would.

Jessie came over and slid into the booth next to Kelly. She swiped one of Zack's french fries, giving him a saucy grin. "Yum," she said, chewing appreciatively. "Thanks."

Zack pushed the rest of the fries across the table. "Go ahead and finish them."

Jessie gave him an incredulous look. "You're sharing your fries? Are you sure you feel okay?" She looked at the fries suspiciously. "You don't have a contagious disease or anything, do you?"

"I'm just being generous with my best friend," Zack said with a smile.

"Uh-oh," Jessie said, adding more catsup to the plate. "Now I *know* something's wrong."

"I'm just glad to see you," Zack protested. "You haven't been around much lately. You're always with the Hollywood Hills crowd."

"Not always," Jessie said. "I still go to Bayside, you know. But I *am* having a lot of fun."

"Good," Zack said. How was he going to ruin this perfectly good conversation? he wondered. Kelly was shooting him encouraging looks from across the table. "That's good," he repeated. "But how well do you really *know* these kids, Jess?"

"They're so open and friendly. I feel like I've known them for years," Jessie said enthusiastically. She popped a french fry in her mouth.

This wasn't going very well, Zack thought in despair. "New friendships are the blossoms on the tree of life," he said. *Terrific. Now he was sounding like a greeting card.* "But not every blossom bears fruit."

"Right on, O great guru," Jessie said, giggling. "But what are you talking about?"

"I'm saying that this new crowd might not be what they seem," Zack blurted.

Jessie put down her french fry and wiped her fingers on a napkin. "You're talking about Star, aren't you," she said evenly.

Zack nodded. "Are you sure you can trust her? Don't you think she's coming on kind of strong? And Kelly says she was a really hot item with Thunder just a couple of weeks ago."

Jessie shot Kelly a furious look. "For your information, Star already told me that," she said icily. "And she has absolutely no interest in Thunder anymore. They're just friends. Like . . . like me and Slater."

"Right," Zack said. "Like you and Slater. Come on, Jessie."

"It's true," Jessie said angrily. "Star is a really nice person. She just invited me to a superbig party—"

"I heard," Zack said quietly. "And she also suggested that your best friend lie for you so you can go. Jessie, you wouldn't have done that if it wasn't for Star."

"Kelly doesn't have to do it," Jessie said defensively. "We can just forget it."

"Jessie, it's not just that. I'm worried about you," Kelly said in a soft voice.

Jessie stood up. "Look," she said. "I'm having *fun* with these kids. They don't have any expectations about who Jessie Spano is. I can be any way I want to be. I don't have to be the smart one, the serious one. Nobody teases me about reading too many books or going on too many protest marches. They just accept me."

"But they don't really know you," Zack pointed out. "You *do* read a lot of books. You *do* care about causes."

Jessie's hands clenched into fists. "Well, maybe they don't know all of me," she said. She fixed Zack and then Kelly with furious hazel eyes. "But maybe you guys don't, either."

Jessie strode out of the Max. Zack picked up a french fry and put it down again. He sighed. "I'm sorry, Kelly. I think I made things worse."

"It's okay, Zack," Kelly said softly. "You tried."

"I feel terrible," Zack admitted. "Jessie's really mad at me. I wish I *had* been wearing the blindfold so I didn't actually have to see it."

Kelly's hand crept across the table and slipped into his. "Don't worry, Zack," she said. "Jessie will come around. And we can talk it all over tonight."

"Right," Zack said. He sighed again.

Kelly prodded him gently with her sneaker underneath the table. "When we go to the little café down the coast," she said softly.

Zack barely heard her. "Yeah."

"Just you and me."

Slowly, Zack began to grin. "At the beach."

Kelly giggled. "Under a full moon."

Zack waggled his eyebrows. "Alone."

"At the beach."

Girls' Night Out   85

"Just you and me."

"Under a full moon."

"Just you and—" But Zack didn't get a chance to finish. Kelly leaned over and kissed him. Now, that beat a cold french fry any day.

Chapter 9

▲ ▼ ▲ ▼ ▲ ▼ ▲

Zack called Slater before dinner and outlined what had happened at the Max that day.

"Maybe she'll listen to you," Zack told him. "We just think she should be careful with this crowd. You know that Jessie's really sensitive at heart."

"Jessie listen to me?" Slater asked. "You must be hallucinating. She's got a head harder than Pinocchio. And once she gets ahold of something, she's like a sumo wrestler. And last of all, I don't agree with you about Star. I know she seems like she's in the fast lane, but she's a nice girl. You guys don't know her."

"Mmmm, maybe," Zack said noncommittally. "But I wish Jessie wouldn't go to that party. I have a bad feeling about it."

Slater thought for a minute. "I'll tell you what. I

can keep an eye on Jessie at the party. Make sure she gets back to Kelly's on time. Star is probably going to invite me tonight."

"All right," Zack said grudgingly. "I guess I feel better knowing you're going to be there, too. But I'm telling you, Jessie's heading for trouble."

Slater sighed. "We've all got troubles, Zack."

"What do you mean?" Zack asked. He heard the sad note in Slater's voice. He and Kelly had thought that Slater's bad mood was because he was pining over Jessie and wouldn't admit it. But maybe something else was going on. "What's happening, buddy?"

"Nothing. Listen, my parents just got home. See you at school tomorrow." Slater hung up the phone. He wasn't ready to talk to his friends until he knew for sure what was wrong. Straightening his shoulders, he headed downstairs to face the music.

His parents were sitting in the living room, holding hands. Slater would have taken that as a good sign, except he figured that if his parents *were* getting a divorce, they'd be all modern and civilized about it.

"We brought back tacos," his mother said. "They're in the oven, keeping warm. We thought we'd have our talk first."

Slater sat down on the ottoman. "Look, just do me a favor, okay? Don't beat around the bush. If it's bad news, just tell me."

"It's not—" his father started.

Slater closed his eyes. "Just give it to me straight."

"I'm going to have a baby," his mother said.

Slater opened his eyes. His mother was smiling softly. Her face still looked pale, but her eyes were shining. His mouth dropped open. "You're going to *what*?"

"Maybe I should say *we're* going to have a baby," his mother said, glancing at his father. "All of us. Because it's going to affect all of us."

"B-but, wait a minute," Slater sputtered. "Aren't you too *old*?"

His mother raised an eyebrow at him.

"What I meant was," Slater babbled quickly, "you don't *look* too old, but do you want . . . I mean, did you think . . . "

Grinning, his father saved him. "No, we didn't plan it, but it happened. And we're really happy about it."

"Is that why you've been so tired and mopey?" Slater asked his mother.

She nodded. "I'm having a rough first trimester. I'm sleepy all the time, and I get morning sickness morning, noon, and night. But the doctor said it should pass in a couple of weeks."

"Was that appointment you two were going to this afternoon for the doctor?" Slater asked shrewdly.

"We wanted to make sure everything was still okay before we told you," his mother said.

"So is this why you've been looking so worried?" Slater asked his father. He felt like he had a million questions. He was so relieved, he felt like dancing across the room.

"We *were* a little worried at first," his father said. "Happy—and worried. Having a baby is expensive. And that's what we wanted to talk to you about, son. Things might be tight around here for a bit. Your mom will have to take a leave of absence from work when the baby's born. We might have to dip into the money we saved for your college."

"I understand," Slater said happily. "I'll help out, don't worry. I'll have a brother or sister. Wow, thanks, you guys."

His mother laughed. "So it's okay?"

"Okay? It's fantastic!" Slater said. He sprang up and kissed his mother and hugged his father. "I'm completely psyched!"

His mother had tears in her eyes. "Me, too," she said, grinning.

"Let's hit the kitchen," his father said. "We don't want incinerated tacos, do we?"

"I forgot all about dinner," Slater said, leading the way.

His mother laughed. "You *really* must be in shock," she said.

Slater couldn't believe it. This was the most awesome news he'd ever had. He could hardly wait to tell Star all about it.

▲   ▼   ▲

"Whew," Star said, sliding into Slater's car. "You won't *believe* what happened. Morticia raided my closet *again*. She borrowed my brand-new linen jacket to wear out to dinner with my dad. She'll probably dribble bat-wing juice on it or something. And then when I got home from the beach, she was monopolizing the StairMaster. I'm going to make Daddy buy me my own. This is ridiculous. Three people just can't share a gym. Now, there's a perfectly good guest room that's never used on the third floor, and he could hire a designer like that," she snapped her fingers, "who could make it into a gym just for me in nothing flat. Don't you think that's a good idea?"

"Sure," Slater said. "Do you want to go to Eddie's?" he asked, naming a café Star liked.

Star shrugged. "Anywhere. Just get me away from *here*. I hate Pam, I really do."

"Pam?"

"Morticia," Star explained. "She is *soooo* selfish."

"I had that meeting with my parents tonight," Slater reminded her. He didn't think he should *have* to remind her, but maybe she was really upset about her stepmother.

"Mmmm," Star said. "You know, yesterday I just know she used my very own phone to make a call. The whole receiver just *reeked* of Shalimar. It was totally gross. I sprayed it with Lysol."

"Yuk," Slater said, to be polite. He tried again. "So at this talk, my parents finally told me what was wrong."

"Oh, right. So, are they getting divorced, or what?" Star asked. She tilted the rearview mirror toward her so that she could check her lipstick.

"No," Slater said, tilting it back so that he could see the tailgating car behind him. "But the family *is* changing. I'm getting a brother or sister!" he announced proudly.

"Wow," Star said. "Congratulations, I guess."

"Thanks," Slater said. He was relieved that Star had finally become interested. For a minute, he'd felt pretty badly when she hadn't asked what had happened. "I'm completely psyched," he added.

"Just wait until Junior gets here," Star said, getting a small pocket mirror out of her purse and squinting into it. "Pretty soon, he'll be getting in your hair, and you'll wish you were an only child again. Personally, I'm *thrilled* to be an only child. I always tell Daddy, please, please, do *not* give me a brother or sister. I can do without one, I assure you. Especially if they're related to Pam."

Star went off again on how selfish Pam was and how she couldn't *believe* that Pam didn't want her along when Pam and her father went to the Cannes Film Festival in a few weeks. So what if Star had to miss school? She was *smart*, for heaven's sakes, and half her class was going. Well, she knew of at least *two* people who were going with their parents, and they weren't even staying in the right hotel. And would Slater mind if they went home early? She had a super amount of homework. Come to think of it, she was going to be absolutely *crazed* for a while, so she really wouldn't be available.

Slater couldn't believe it. Star wasn't interested in him anymore at all. She hadn't even asked him to the party. It was pretty clear that she was dumping him, and she'd just come out tonight because she had had to. He could have floated out of the car and off into the night, and she wouldn't even have noticed.

Zack and Kelly were right. The reason Star *seemed* like a shallow, superficial girl was because she was one!

Slater frowned as he pulled into the parking lot of Eddie's. Now he was worried, too. Knowing how openhearted Jessie was, wasn't she bound to get hurt?

▲   ▼   ▲

That night, Jessie packed her overnight bag and went over to Kelly's. She could hardly look at her mother when she said good-bye, and she could hardly look at Kelly when she arrived. It wasn't easy to be a risk taker, she decided.

Kelly had told her parents that she, Zack, and Jessie were all going to the movies together. They climbed into the car, Jessie carrying a leather tote bag filled with her dress-up clothes, makeup, and shoes. They were all silent as they drove to the beach, where Jessie was supposed to meet Thunder.

Jessie got out of the car. It was foggy at the beach, and the cold wind raised goose bumps on her arms. She leaned in the window and met Kelly's honest blue eyes. Jessie's glance slid away, and she checked the parking lot for Thunder's Porsche. "I'll meet you at the Max at midnight," she said.

"Don't be late," Kelly said.

"I won't," Jessie said. "I promise. And, thanks. You're a true pal, Kelly. I'll never ask you to do anything like this again. It's too nerve-racking."

"I'll say," Kelly said ruefully. "I just hope my parents don't find out. Have a good time."

"Right," Zack echoed. "Have fun."

Jessie looked at her two friends. "Do you really mean it?"

Kelly tried to smile. "If we're going to all this trouble, you'd *better* have a good time."

Jessie smiled faintly. "Thanks," she said.

Zack's car took off, and Jessie ran to the beach bathroom. She brushed out her long hair until it waved around her face in a riot of soft curls. Then she slipped into the silver tunic minidress and matching spangled tights she'd brought. Lisa had helped her pick out the outfit and had talked her into a pair of high-heeled ankle boots and dangling earrings. They were much more dramatic than the accessories Jessie usually wore, but after all, she was a new person.

Jessie peered into the cracked mirror. She looked okay, she decided. Maybe not movie-star material, but she'd do. She added some lipstick and shoved her jeans and T-shirt into the tote bag and she was ready.

Thunder was waiting outside, looking spectacular in loose-fitting gray pants, a matching jacket, and a white washed-silk shirt.

"You look great," Jessie said. "I love your suit."

"Armani," Thunder said. "Star helped me pick it out a couple of months ago. C'mon, we'd better jam."

He took her arm and led her to his Porsche. Jessie felt like a queen as she slid into the front seat and tucked her legs in.

"How has your week gone?" she asked Thunder as he headed for the freeway.

"Super. Fantastic surf, lots of workable rides.

I had a killer rush today, man. It was my last ride, and—"

Jessie kept a smile plastered to her face as Thunder went on to describe his surfing afternoon in minute detail. *Smiling is key*, Lisa had told her. *Especially when you're bored to tears*. Not that she was bored right now, Jessie amended quickly.

Actually, it was a *relief* not to have to match wits with someone every single second. And even though when Thunder started talking, Jessie wanted to nod out, it had to be because she was so relaxed. Not bored.

When they got to Star's huge Tudor mansion, Jessie gasped. There must have been thousands of tiny white lights strung through the branches of the trees and shrubs. It looked like a fairy-tale castle. This was definitely going to be a magical evening, she just knew it!

A uniformed valet opened the car door. A butler checked Thunder's engraved invitation. Pots of blooming flowers lined the impressive entry hall, and Jessie spotted the star of her favorite sitcom. She was about to tell Thunder when she noticed Star heading down the stairs, smiling at them. She looked gorgeous in a very short black satin dress and matching high-heeled pumps.

"You look like a movie star," Jessie told her.

Star laughed. "Thanks. One of these days, I'd like to be."

"You want to be an actress?" Jessie asked.

Star nodded. "It's my dream. Come on, let's find the gang and get some food."

"Now you're talking," Thunder said.

For the next few hours, Jessie felt like she was in a movie. Every time she turned around, she saw another famous face. She was content just to look, too nervous to say hello to anyone. It wouldn't be cool, she felt sure, to gush all over her favorite stars. But nobody, famous or not famous, talked to her, anyway. Even Star was busy flitting from guest to guest, and Thunder was talking surf and sports cars with the rest of the guys from the crowd.

Jessie started to feel hot and just the teensiest bit bored. It was pretty crazy to feel bored at an exclusive Hollywood party, but she thought of how much more fun it would be if Slater, Zack, Lisa, Screech, and Kelly were here to talk about it with.

Finally, Jessie wandered outside to the garden for air. It was empty, and she sniffed the fragrant night air, glad for the cool breeze. She wondered if it was too early for her to ask Thunder to take her back to Palisades.

"Hiding—or getting some air?" A man about her father's age, with an amiable-looking face and horn-rimmed glasses, walked toward her. He held out his hand. "Raymond Tobin."

"Jessie Spano," Jessie said, shaking his hand. "And maybe I'm doing some of both."

He laughed. "Actress?"

Jessie shook her head.

"Model, then."

Jessie grinned. "Student. Do you always talk in shorthand, Mr. Tobin?"

He laughed. "Actually, yes. I'm a screenwriter, so maybe it comes from that."

"A screenwriter?" Jessie said. "How wonderful. What have you written?"

"A movie nobody saw," he said with a rueful grin. "Called *Tomorrow's Children*."

"I can't believe it!" Jessie exclaimed. "*I* saw it. I loved it."

"How do you like that," Ray Tobin said. "I get invited to an *A*-list party and meet the only person in America who saw my movie. This is quite a night."

Jessie laughed. She found herself liking Raymond Tobin. At last she'd found someone who liked to *talk*, not just stand around and pose.

She found herself talking to Raymond Tobin as if she'd known him forever. He'd been a college professor who'd gone into screenwriting. Star's father was his agent, but he felt Mr. Craven might drop him soon if he didn't sell another script. And he asked about Jessie, too. When Ray Tobin finally looked at his watch and said he had to go, she couldn't believe it was past eleven.

Ray Tobin shook her hand good-bye. "Funny,"

he said. "You're nothing like Star."

"I know," Jessie said ruefully.

"I said that as a compliment," he returned lightly, but before she could ask him what he meant, he said a last good-bye and headed down the path toward his car.

Jessie went back inside to look for Thunder. She went from room to room, but she couldn't find him anywhere. She didn't see Star, either. Suddenly, all the glittering rooms were full of strangers. Beginning to get worried, she started to look all over again. Finally, she saw Mr. Craven deep in conversation by the huge marble fireplace.

"Hi, Mr. Craven," she said. "It's Jessie Spano, Star's friend. I'm sorry to interrupt, but have you seen her or Thunder?"

"They went to get some pizza, I think," Mr. Craven said. He turned to his companion. "My daughter thinks that caviar and smoked salmon from Scotland are, like, totally gross."

The man laughed. "Have to keep up with the youth market, Greg. Speaking of which . . ."

The two men went back to their conversation and ignored Jessie completely. She stood in the middle of the room while guests swirled around her. She felt like bursting into tears. The whole gang had left without her. And it was getting close to Kelly's curfew. What was she going to do?

Chapter 10

▲ ▼ ▲ ▼ ▲ ▼ ▲

Jessie tried not to panic. She tried not to think about what would happen if she didn't show up at the Max on time. She dashed back out to the garden and down the path Mr. Tobin had taken toward the cars, which were parked in the back. She scanned the lot anxiously, but Mr. Tobin had left. Thunder's Porsche was gone, too.

Biting her lip, Jessie glanced back at the house. There was no one she could call to come and get her. Zack and Kelly were probably still at the movies, and, anyway, there wasn't enough time for someone to drive to Hollywood and get her back to Palisades on time. She didn't have enough money for a cab.

There was only one thing to do. Setting her chin

grimly, Jessie headed down the long, curving driveway toward the main road . . . and the bus.

▲   ▼   ▲

Kelly glanced anxiously at the Max's wall clock. "It's five to twelve," she said. "We're already going to be late getting home."

"She'll be here," Zack said. His fingers drummed nervously on the seat next to him, where Kelly couldn't see. He was nervous, too.

"Stop drumming your fingers, Zack," Kelly said. "You're making me nervous."

"How about another soda?" Zack suggested.

"I've already had two colas," Kelly said. "If I have another one, I'll float right out the door. Besides, I'm sure Jessie's about to walk right in."

"Right," Zack said.

Kelly sighed. "How about root beer this time?"

▲   ▼   ▲

"It's twelve-thirty, Zack," Kelly said. Her dark blue eyes were full of concern. "I don't know whether to be mad or worried."

"It's not like Jessie, that's for sure," Zack said. "But, then again, *Jessie* hasn't been like Jessie lately."

"My parents are going to flip," Kelly said. "I'm definitely pushing the edge of the envelope here."

"Kelly, I have an idea," Zack said. "Why don't I take you home? You can cover for Jessie while I look around Palisades for her. I'll keep checking back here. When she comes, we'll throw pebbles at your window and you can sneak her in."

"But what about your curfew?" Kelly asked. "Your parents are almost as uptight as mine are."

"Don't worry about me," Zack assured her. "I'll handle it. I couldn't go home until I knew that she was safe and sound, anyway. So come on." He smiled and brushed a lock of dark hair off Kelly's forehead. "Trust me," he said.

▲   ▼   ▲

Jessie hugged her boots to her chest and walked down the dark street, barefoot. Her feet were killing her, and she had never felt so tired. It was almost two in the morning. She'd never dreamed it would take so long to get back. But then again, she'd never dreamed it would take three buses and a two-mile walk through the streets of Palisades.

Jessie paused. A dark form was rising out of a car down the street. A man. Now he was heading toward her. He broke into a run!

She whirled around. Panic gave her new strength, and she started to run, too.

"Jessie! Jessie!"

Jessie stopped. She doubted that a mugger would know her name. She peered through the darkness. "Zack? Oh, Zack, I'm so glad it's you." She burst into tears and leaned on his shoulder.

"What happened to you?" Zack asked with anger and concern in his voice.

"I was stranded at the party," Jessie said. "So I took the bus. The first one broke down, and then I took the wrong connection back to Palisades and wound up outside of town. I've been walking for an hour."

"Come on," Zack said. "We'd better get to Kelly's. Let's hope we can still sneak in."

But when they got to Kelly's, any thoughts of sneaking in were squashed when they saw that the living-room lights were blazing.

"Oh, gosh," Jessie said. "I'm in for it now."

Mr. Kapowski opened the front door. "Come on in, Jessie," he said.

Jessie walked nervously past him and into the living room. Mrs. Kapowski and Kelly were waiting, looking strained and exhausted.

"Thank heaven," Mrs. Kapowski said, and Kelly burst into tears.

"I'm so sorry," Jessie whispered.

"She had to take the bus," Zack explained. "She made the wrong connection, and she got lost."

"Kelly," Mrs. Kapowski said, "I think you and

Jessie should go up to bed. We'll talk about all this in the morning. Zack should get home. Zack, your mother's waiting for you."

"Does my mother know?" Jessie asked.

"No," Mrs. Kapowski said. Her blue eyes, usually so kind, were stern. "We didn't want to worry her yet. But I think you realize, Jessie, that I'm going to have to call her tomorrow and tell her."

"I know," Jessie said. Her voice was barely audible. Kelly said good-night to everyone and led her upstairs. They brushed their teeth and washed their faces and slipped into the cool sheets in silence.

"I'm really sorry, Kelly," Jessie said. "I know I got you into awful trouble."

"I just hope that now you realize what that crowd is like," Kelly murmured. "Nobody cared how you were going to get home."

"I know," Jessie said. She flipped over in bed and stared out the window into the dark night. Kelly might be right. But Jessie couldn't help hoping that Star or Thunder would have some sort of explanation.

▲   ▼   ▲

Jessie left Kelly's house early. She apologized to Mr. and Mrs. Kapowski again, but she could see they were still upset with her. As soon as she left, she knew they would have a serious talk with Kelly. Mrs. Kapowski had already called her mother. Jessie figured that tonight she might be sleeping in Domino's doghouse.

Instead, she got grounded and assigned a month's worth of yard work. Jessie accepted her punishment without a word of complaint. Even worse than the anger was the disappointment in her mother's eyes.

"I'm furious at you," Mrs. Spano told her, "but I'm also confused and hurt. *And* worried. What's happening to you, Jessie?"

Jessie sighed as she weeded the garden. She felt just as confused as her mother did. In the past week, she'd had a party behind her mother's back and lied to her. She'd even asked her best friends to lie for her. What *was* happening to her?

A shadow fell over her hands as she tugged at a stubborn weed. Jessie looked up. Star was standing over her, a contrite expression on her face.

"I feel terrible," Star said dramatically. "I deserve to be locked away and the key to be thrown into a bottomless pit." She sank onto the grass next to Jessie. "I had no *idea* you were still at the party. My father told me this morning. It's all my fault, too—don't blame Thunder for a second. Jessie, I *swear* to you I looked everywhere for you. Then I bumped into Ray Tobin and he told me that you'd gone home. I asked *how*, of course, but he didn't know."

"That's funny," Jessie said. "I *was* talking to Mr. Tobin, but he went straight to his car to go home."

"He must have come back into the house," Star said. "We must have just missed you inside. Jessie, can you ever, ever forgive me?" Star looked so distraught Jessie had to forgive her. Part of her thought that it would have been nice for Star to look for her just a little bit harder. But Star seemed truly upset now.

"There's nothing to forgive," Jessie said. "It was just a misunderstanding."

"Did I get you in terrible trouble?" Star asked.

"Well, at first I was grounded for the next fifty years," Jessie said with a laugh. "But now it's only for two weekends."

"That means you won't be able to see Thunder," Star said, aghast. "Oh, Jessie, I am lower than a snake's belly."

Jessie couldn't help laughing. "Don't worry about it," she said. "I'll survive."

Star suddenly clapped a hand to her mouth. "Oh, no!" she exclaimed. "I just thought of something. I hope being grounded doesn't mean you can't do something next Saturday?"

"Depends," Jessie said. "I'm not grounded during the day, just at night."

"Good," Star said in relief. "Because Daddy just

told me the most incredible news. You know ROCK-TV, the music video channel? They're having a citywide contest to pick two high school students, a girl and a guy, to do a guest VJ spot for a whole week! The tryouts are next Saturday. You've just *got* to try out, Jessie. You already have experience since you've been a DJ at your school."

"But what about you?" Jessie asked. "Don't you want to try out? If you want to be an actress, it would be great exposure, right?"

Star shrugged. "I just don't think I have the right stuff for this. I don't know very much about music. But you're perfect, Jessie! And here's the best part—Daddy is a friend of one of the producers. We can find out what type they're looking for, and then I'll coach you. You can be that type!"

"Is that fair?" Jessie asked.

"Fair, schmair," Star said, waving a hand. Then she saw the frown on Jessie's face. "Everyone does it, Jessie. Everyone in L.A., anyway. You've just *got* to have an angle, Daddy says it all the time. I can coach Kelly and Lisa, too. You'll all have a fair shot."

"Well, okay," Jessie said. "Maybe the guys at Bayside will want to try out. I'll have to tell Zack about it. He's always ready for anything."

"I guess Slater will be too busy preparing for the new baby to do it," Star said idly.

Jessie's head jerked. "What?"

"The new baby. His mom is pregnant. Didn't you know?"

Jessie felt a pang seize her heart. "No," she said slowly. "He didn't tell me."

"Oh. Listen, I've gotta jam. I'm meeting the kids at the beach. I wish you could come." Star sprang up and dusted off her cutoffs. "I'll call you as soon as I hear more about the contest!"

Jessie waved good-bye to Star. She returned thoughtfully to her weeding. She was glad to know that there was a good explanation about last night. But she didn't feel as relieved and happy as she thought she would have. Instead, she wondered why Slater hadn't told her about the baby. Jessie had thought she'd never feel as left out as she had last night, when she realized she was stranded. But right now, she felt even worse.

▲   ▼   ▲

Kelly couldn't bear the atmosphere at her house any longer. Even her brothers and sisters were playing quietly. When someone was in trouble at the Kapowskis, everyone felt it. Finally, Kelly just had to pull on her running shoes and head for the park for a nice long jog. She had to forget how awful she felt at letting her parents down.

But the escape she craved was foiled when she

saw Thunder at the jogging track. His bronze chest was bare, and his long blond hair was held back with a bandanna. He jogged up to her when he saw her.

"Hey. Kathy, right?"

"Kelly," she said shortly. She sure wasn't about to be friendly to a guy who'd left her friend stranded at a party. Besides, Thunder had met her three or four times. It was pretty rude of him not to remember her name.

"Kelly, right. How's it going?"

"Great," Kelly said. *Why am I being nice to this creep*? she wondered to herself. *Because you're too nice*, she could hear Zack telling her. If the guy is a creep, shouldn't someone *tell* him he's a creep?

Kelly spun around to face him. "Actually," she said, "I'm real upset about my friend. It seems she got stranded by her date at a big Hollywood party. She had to take three buses home in the middle of the night. It was lucky something didn't happen to her."

"Wow," Thunder said, shaking his blond head. "That's rough."

"You bet it is, buster," Kelly said. "And if Jessie's smart, she'll never forgive you."

"Jessie? You're talking about Jessie?" Thunder looked puzzled.

"Of course I'm talking about Jessie!" Kelly yelled in exasperation.

"Wait a second," Thunder said. Kelly could see realization slowly dawn in his blank blue eyes. "Jessie didn't take a cab home? That's what Star told me."

"What exactly did Star tell you?" Kelly asked, suddenly alert.

Thunder thought a minute. "That her dad told her that Jessie felt sick so he sent her home in a cab. Isn't that what happened?"

"No, it's not what happened at all," Kelly snapped. "Maybe you should have tried a little harder to find out the truth."

"Whoa. This is a killer wipeout, man. I guess I should call Jessie and, like, say I'm sorry or something. I'll catch Star at the beach later and ask her what the story is."

"Sounds like a good idea," Kelly said. "Especially the apology part."

He patted her shoulder. "Thanks, Keely."

"Kelly!" Kelly spun on her heel and jogged away. Had Star lied? she wondered. Or had Thunder been confused or Mr. Craven mistaken? Whatever happened, Kelly vowed to get to the bottom of it. The answer just might convince Jessie that Star Craven was no friend of hers.

Chapter 11

▲ ▼ ▲ ▼ ▲ ▼ ▲

After school on Monday, Jessie hurried through the halls, looking for Slater. She hadn't seen him all day, and she wanted to congratulate him.

"Jessie!" Kelly hurried up to her. "There you are. Are you coming to the shower?"

"Gosh, I took one this morning," Jessie said. "Do you think I need another one already?"

Kelly laughed. "Slater's baby shower, silly. Didn't Zack or Lisa or Screech tell you? We're throwing him a surprise shower in Room three thirteen. Mr. Belding said okay."

"I haven't seen anyone all day," Jessie admitted. "A surprise shower sounds like a great idea." And she should have come up with the idea herself, Jessie thought with a sigh.

She hurried alongside an excited Kelly to the

third floor. The classroom was festooned with streamers, and gaily wrapped presents were stacked on the desk. There were sodas and a bowl of popcorn and bags of pretzels and chips.

"I don't have a present," Jessie said to Kelly.

"Don't worry about it," Kelly said. "They're just joke gifts, from all of us."

"Kelly and I picked them out at the drugstore," Lisa said with a giggle. "We gift wrapped a bunch of diapers and a doll so he can get plenty of practice."

"I picked out the doll," Screech said proudly.

"Shhhh," Zack warned them. "Slater will be here any second. He thinks there's a meeting for the wrestling team."

Zack switched off the lights. It was an overcast day, and the room was instantly sunk into gloom.

A moment later, the door opened. "Hey, what happened to the lights?" Slater wondered aloud. He felt along the wall for the switch and turned it on.

"Surprise!" they all yelled.

Slater jumped back in surprise. "What do you mean, surprise? It's not my birthday!"

"It's a baby shower," Kelly said.

Slater grinned. "You guys are crazy. This is the stupidest thing I ever heard of. Hey—food! This is a great idea!"

Soon the classroom was littered with pink and

blue wrapping paper as Slater tore through the gifts. His expression grew more and more comically disgusted as he unwrapped one diaper after another.

"Get used to them, Slater," Kelly said, laughing. "You're going to be seeing a lot of them." With six brothers and sisters, Kelly had had plenty of practice.

"Me, change a diaper?" Slater made a face. "No way. I'll send the kid to the dry cleaners."

Jessie laughed along with everybody else. They all knew that Slater would be the best big brother in the world.

"I guess you'll be too busy practicing with your doll to go to the VJ contest on Saturday," Zack said.

"Are you kidding? I'm there," Slater said. Then he grinned and crooked the doll's arm over his. "I take my new girl everywhere," he said.

"You've finally met someone who's really perfect for you," Jessie said. "She can't talk, let alone think." Then Slater looked at her, and she blushed and turned away. She had meant the remark as a joke, of course, but there had been an edge in her voice, and Slater had heard it.

In order to change the subject, she turned quickly to Kelly and Lisa. "Are you guys going to try out? I am."

"You are?" Zack asked, surprised.

"Really?" Lisa said.

Jessie flushed angrily. "Why not?"

"It's not really your thing, Jessie," Kelly explained. "You said once that music videos are turning the brains of American teens to mush."

"Well, I changed my mind," Jessie said. "I'm allowed to, aren't I?"

"Sure," Kelly said.

"Star's father knows the producer," Jessie said. "His name is Sylvester York, and he's coming to dinner at the Cravens on Wednesday. She's going to ask what type they're looking for. Then she offered to coach all of us. Isn't that nice of her? She really knows the TV industry because of her father."

Kelly stared at Jessie in disbelief. "Are you still *friends* with Star?" she asked.

"After she dumped you at that party?" Lisa asked.

"She explained all that," Jessie said quickly. "She said she was really sorry. She asked this writer I was talking to if he'd seen me, and he told her that I'd taken a cab home. Weird, huh?"

"Totally," Kelly said dryly. "Especially when Thunder told me that Star told *him* that her father told *her* that you'd felt sick and he sent you home in a cab. She should get her stories straight. Didn't Thunder call you to apologize?"

Jessie frowned. "No. I didn't hear from him all day Sunday. I'm sure you're confused, Kelly."

Kelly shook her head. "No way."

"Then Thunder is," Jessie said flatly.

"I don't think so, Jessie," Kelly said. "I think Star lied to you."

Jessie sprang up angrily. "I don't believe you're going into this again, Kelly. Can't you just accept that Star and I have become friends?"

"I'm sure you're her friend," Kelly said in the same steady voice. "But I'm not sure about Star."

"Well, *I'm* sure," Jessie said. "Maybe if you'd get over being jealous, you would be, too."

Kelly opened her mouth to snap back, but Zack stepped forward, right onto her foot.

"Ow!" she protested. She felt her toes gingerly. It was a wonder they weren't flat as little pancakes. Zack was wearing his hiking boots today.

"Sorry, Kelly," Zack said, oozing sincerity.

Kelly's eyes narrowed. She could tell he had done it deliberately. Her scalp was tingling, and every nerve was jumping. Whenever that happened, it was a sign that Zack was up to something again. Years of practice had taught Kelly the warning signs. The first one was when Zack suddenly became very, *very* nice.

"That's really terrific of Star to help you girls out," Zack said. "I think you and Lisa should take her up on it, Kelly."

"You do?" Kelly asked.

"You do?" Lisa asked.

"You do?" Jessie asked.

"Absolutely," Zack said.

Kelly and Lisa exchanged puzzled looks. Kelly couldn't imagine what was going on in Zack's scheming brain. But as Zack casually asked Jessie for more details, she was even more convinced that something was definitely cooking. Her scalp wasn't just tingling anymore, and her nerves weren't just jumping—they were doing the funky chicken!

▲   ▼   ▲

"This will never work," Lisa said.

"Yes, it will," Zack said for the umpteenth time.

"I don't know, Zack," Kelly said doubtfully. She worriedly looked around the downtown L.A. coffee shop. "Maybe we should just go home."

"Trust me," Zack said. "Aren't we getting an *A* on our science project because I trust *you*? It's your turn now."

"I never would have thought up that stupid project if I'd known you would throw it back in my face," Kelly grumbled.

"You see, Kelly, you should have *trusted* that Zack would throw it back in your face," Screech said matter-of-factly. "Hand me the phone, will you? I have to call my agent."

"You don't have an agent, Screech," Lisa said.

Screech's head bobbed in agreement. "I know. That's why I have to call around and find one. I think I could make a success out of this."

"Whoa," Zack said. "Let's have a reality check here, Screech. You're *impersonating* a TV producer. You are really a high school student."

Screech admired himself in the mirror over the table. "I'm a prodigy," he told his reflection lovingly.

They had all helped devise Screech's outfit over the past few days. He was wearing a suit of Zack's, which they hoped draped fashionably around his thin frame. Slater had lent him his coolest pair of sunglasses and wished him luck because he couldn't be there. He had to take his mom to the doctor. Lisa had added a paisley silk scarf—a perfect Hollywood touch.

But the final touch was the best—Zack had borrowed his father's portable phone. He just hoped his father wouldn't notice.

Now he snatched the phone away from Screech. "If you make any calls on this, you're gerbil food," he warned.

"Gerbils are vegetarians," Screech informed him loftily.

"They'll change," Zack snarled.

"I don't know about this," Lisa sighed. "I'd feel better if Zack or Slater were impersonating Sylvester York."

"You know they can't," Kelly said worriedly.

"Star talked to both of them. We're hoping she won't remember Screech."

Zack looked at his watch. "You'd better get moving, Lisa. It's time."

"Right." Lisa moved to the back, where the phone booths were. She would call Sylvester York at the station, pretending to be Mr. Craven's secretary, and cancel the dinner. She'd already called Star earlier that day, pretending to be Sylvester York's secretary, and told her he couldn't make the dinner but would meet her for a few minutes in a coffee shop near the ROCK-TV offices.

"Everything should work perfectly," Zack told Kelly and Screech nervously as they watched Lisa in the phone booth.

"*Should* is the scary part," Kelly said. "What if it doesn't?"

Just then, the door of the phone booth opened and Lisa emerged. She gave them a thumbs-up sign. "Time for phase two," she announced.

"We still have a few minutes," Zack said. "I'm hungry." He looked around for the waitress and saw Star walk into the coffee shop. She hadn't seen him, thank goodness. Zack immediately slid down onto the floor of the booth.

"I know I dropped my tomato down there, Zack, but I'm sure the waitress will bring you another one," Screech said, bending down to talk to him.

"Shhh!" Zack tugged on Kelly's skirt and yanked on Lisa's elbow. "Star's here! She's early!"

Kelly and Lisa went flat on the seat of the booth. "What should we do?" Kelly hissed.

"Screech, go up and introduce yourself to Star," Zack murmured rapidly. "Make sure and keep her back to us. We'll go out the back way."

Screech slid out of the booth with difficulty, trying to get over Lisa's head.

"Ouch," Lisa muttered. "That's my hair."

"Sorry, Lisa," Screech moaned. "Gosh, I feel awful. I always said I'd never harm a hair on your head."

"Get moving," Zack whispered fiercely. "And be cool!"

Screech sprang off the end of the seat, tripped over Zack, whose long legs stuck out from underneath the table, and went sprawling forward into the coffee shop in a series of trips and slips, almost-tumbles and near-stumbles, until he took a header and landed right at Star's feet.

Zack let out a low groan. He should have known better than to advise Screech to be cool!

"Stay down, Zack," Kelly muttered.

"How are we going to get out of here?" Lisa fretted.

"I'm getting a crick in my neck," Kelly said.

"My hair is completely flat on one side," Lisa whispered.

"Shhhh," Zack warned. He was trying to hear Screech.

"Glad to meet you, babe," Screech said, looking up at Star from the floor. "Sylvester York here."

Star looked down. "I'm glad to meet you, Mr. York," she said.

"Call me Sylvester. Or better yet, Sly." Screech jerked to his feet and straightened his sunglasses. "Did you see where my portable phone went, by the way? I always have to be reachable by my staff. Hollywood never sleeps. Rock on."

Star bent over and picked it up. "Here it is. Should we sit down?" She started toward the back of the coffee shop.

"No!" Screech yelled. Then he cleared his throat. "What I mean is, I'm on this new exercise regime, babe. I never sit down."

Star looked at him, puzzled. "You never sit down?"

"Do you know how many calories you burn standing up? Twenty-five," Screech improvised wildly. "Do you know how many you burn sitting down? Zip. The big oh. Zero."

"I get it," Star said.

Screech gave her a quick once-over. He leaned closer and gave her a wink over his sunglasses. "And we can all stand to burn a few extra calories, can't we, babe?"

"Certainly," Star said, trying not to look offended.

Zack, Kelly, and Lisa heard this exchange. They

had to bury their mouths in Naugahyde to keep from bursting out laughing. It was clear that no one had *ever* told the perfectly fit Star she could stand to burn some calories!

"The other thing I do is hop," Screech said.

"Hop?"

"All the time. It's the newest thing. I go to the best trainer in L.A." Screech began to hop. "You burn *seventy-five* calories this way. I always hop when I take a meeting."

Star began to hop. "Seventy-five calories?"

Ignoring the waitress's rolled eyes, Screech hopped around her and nodded. "By the way, I'm sorry I couldn't make dinner with your father. Great man. Major power broker. But a guy with heart. One of my closest friends. I always say, Gil Craven is—"

"Greg."

"That's what I said. Greg Craven is a player. Now, what do you want to see me about?"

"Well, Mr. York—"

"Sly."

"Sly, I was wondering," Star panted, "if you could give me any tips on the VJ contest. Like what kind of girl you're looking for."

Screech switched to his other foot and hopped. He was getting kind of tired, but Zack had told him to distract Star, and she was definitely distracted. Maybe he was going too far, though. Her face was pretty red. In another minute, she might even pass out. He'd better bring the meeting to a close.

"Sure, Star," he said. "We're looking for that fresh, girl-next-door quality. Open faced, American, apple pie, the flag." Screech saluted. "Innocent, unaffected, unsophisticated."

Star switched to the other foot, breathing hard. "The ingenuc type."

"Exactly. Precisely." Screech's portable phone began to ring, but he ignored it. What if it was a call for Zack's father? Or what if Mr. Morris was calling to find out who had his phone?

"Aren't you going to answer that?" Star asked.

"I really have to run—I mean, hop." Screech started toward the door. "I'll hop you to your car. Let's do lunch."

Star and Screech hopped out of the coffee shop. Kelly, Lisa, and Zack raised their heads cautiously. They grinned at each other across the tabletop.

"It worked!" Kelly exclaimed.

"Amazing," Lisa said, shaking her head. "Screech actually pulled it off."

"Now the rest is up to Star," Zack said.

Chapter 12

▲ ▼ ▲ ▼ ▲ ▼ ▲

On the day of the auditions, Jessie peered at her reflection in Star's full-length mirror. "I don't know," she said hesitantly. "I just don't feel like me."

"You sure don't *look* like you," Kelly said.

"I'll say," Lisa agreed. They were sitting on the love seat in Star's blue-and-silver bedroom. Everything was done in deep blue satin, and stars were painted on the ceiling in the form of Star's zodiac sign. A single huge silver star hung over her bed.

Star stepped back from adjusting a ruffle on the blouse she'd loaned Jessie. "That's the point, girls," she said firmly. "And use your new voice when you talk, Jessie. You need the practice."

"I just don't feel like me," Jessie repeated in the high, breathy voice Star had coached her on.

"Good," Star said. "I told you, Jessie, Sly York told me that they're looking for a real femme fatale type. Sexy and sophisticated."

Jessie looked at her strange reflection again. Black eyeliner rimmed her hazel eyes, and glossy red lipstick was coated on her lips so thickly she felt it might crack any minute. Star had done her long hair so that it flopped over her eye, and stray tendrils kept getting caught in her mascaraed eyelashes. Her skirt was so short and tight she could barely breathe, and the pumps Star had loaned her so that she would walk more sexily made her wobble rather than wiggle.

She wished that she had decided to forgo Star's coaching, like Kelly and Lisa, and just dress like herself. Star herself was wearing bleached jeans, a white linen shirt, and suspenders, and she looked pretty *and* comfortable. It was strange, since Star usually dressed more fashionably and wore more makeup.

"I feel like an idiot," Jessie said. "Are you *sure* I'm what they're looking for? I feel like a cross between Marilyn Monroe and Jessica Rabbit. . . . Speaking of rabbits, Star, why are you hopping?"

Lisa and Kelly bit their lips hard so that they wouldn't laugh. Star was hopping around her bedroom while she picked up her makeup and combs and brushes to put them into her bag. It looked like she'd adopted Screech's exercise routine.

Kelly stood up and yanked Lisa to her feet. "We really should get going. We're meeting the guys at the Max. Jessie, you promised to come, remember?"

Jessie nodded. "I'll be right behind you."

"Don't forget," Kelly said. "Thanks for having us over, Star. We can find the way out."

When the door had closed behind them, Star sighed. "Poor things. In those outfits, they don't have a chance. Now for the finishing touches."

Jessie nodded, resigned. They picked out earrings and sprayed Jessie's hair again. Then Star insisted on *another* coat of lipstick and mascara, and Jessie was done. She said good-bye to Star, promising to meet her at the audition, and tottered down the long upstairs hallway of the Craven house. She practically slid down the staircase, clutching onto the banister for dear life. It was *rough* being a femme fatale, Jessie decided.

As she got into her car, she had a horrible thought. What if she *did* get the VJ slot? She'd have to dress this way for a week! *If* she made it through the whole week, Jessie thought with a shudder. She'd probably fall off these heels and break her neck.

She headed toward the Max, wondering why Kelly and Lisa had been so insistent that she join them there first so that they could all "warm up" before the audition. Nothing would help her warm up, Jessie decided. She was a frozen nervous wreck.

As she drove past Palisades General, she spotted a familiar curly-headed figure heading from the parking lot across the street to the main hospital. Jessie slowed and looked closer. It was Slater. What was he doing there?

Quickly, she eased over to the curb and tapped her horn. When Slater turned, she waved and beckoned. He gave her a quizzical look, then turned back. Jessie honked again, but he kept going.

Jessie leaned out of her window. "Slater! Slater! It's me, Jessie!"

Slater turned and came over slowly. "Sorry, Jess. I didn't recognize you."

"It's my outfit for the audition," Jessie mumbled. "Listen, what's going on? Is everything okay?"

Slater sighed. "Actually, no. My mom lost the baby this morning."

"Oh, Slater," Jessie whispered. "I'm so sorry. Is she okay?"

"Physically, yeah. She's got to stay here for another couple hours, and then she can go home. But she's pretty broken up. So's my dad."

"And what about you?" Jessie asked.

Slater looked over the hood of the car. "Fine. I didn't have that much time to get used to it."

Jessie reached out and covered his hand with her own. "Hey. It's me, Jessie. Talk to me."

He looked back down at her. His mask fell, and

his soft brown eyes were full of pain. "I'm surprised how much it hurts, Jessie."

Jessie switched off her engine. "I'm coming with you," she said. "You need company."

"But what about the audition?"

"Who cares?" *I certainly don't*, Jessie realized. She was sick and tired of trying to be somebody else. It wasn't any fun at all. Who was she kidding? All she got was glazed eyes from having to listen to Thunder, sore feet from wearing heels every day, and a guilty conscience.

Jessie reached for her tote bag in the backseat. It held her jeans, a T-shirt, and sneakers. She could change back into her real self in the rest room and scrub off this stupid makeup.

She slid out of the car and stood next to Slater. She slipped an arm around him. "This is definitely more important," she said. "Come on."

▲   ▼   ▲

After waiting for Jessie as long as they could at the Max, the gang figured she had forgotten. But when they reached the ROCK-TV studio, Jessie wasn't there, either.

"Where can she be?" Lisa wondered.

"This is a disaster," Kelly said. "Now we can't tell her that Star lied to her. She might not have time to change before the audition."

"She'll have time," Zack said. "They've only gone through half the list so far, and she's last."

"We just have to keep an eye on the door," Lisa said. "We've got to grab her as soon as she comes in."

"I wonder where Slater is, too," Kelly said. "Maybe he changed his mind about auditioning."

"I'm so nervous about Jessie, I just know I'm going to blow it," Lisa fretted.

"Me, too," Kelly said. "Look, there's Star. So Jessie isn't with her. Star!" she called, waving her over. When Star came up, she asked, "Have you seen Jessie?"

Star shook her head. "She's not with you? She left my house a half hour ago."

"She's not here yet," Kelly said. "And she never showed up at the Max."

"That's strange," Star said. But she didn't seem too concerned. She looked over at the water cooler, where Screech was taking a drink. "Excuse me, will you? I see someone I know."

"Uh-oh," Lisa murmured. "She still thinks that Screech is a producer."

"Zack Morris!" someone called. "You're up!"

"That was fast," Zack said. "Wish me luck, you guys. And don't forget to watch out for Jessie!"

Over by the water cooler, Screech turned and saw Star advancing on him. He quickly reached into his pocket and slipped on Slater's sunglasses. "Hey, babe, how's it going?" he greeted her.

"Great, Sly. Listen, thanks again for the tip. I guess sometimes it helps knowing the producer."

Star had spoken in a low tone, but a girl standing next to her heard her. She whispered to her girlfriend, and they drifted closer.

"Actually," Star said, "I wanted to talk to you about something. I'm not on the list, so—"

"I see," Screech said. "Not trying out, huh?"

"Actually—"

The two girls came over to them. One pushed the other forward. Sweeping her long blond hair behind her shoulders, the pretty girl giggled and said to Screech, "You're one of the producers?"

"Uh, well . . . ," Screech stammered.

"He's Sylvester York, and I'm having a *private* conversation with him," Star said pointedly.

"Sly York!" The girl moved closer to Screech and took his arm. "I'd love to hear all about how you broke into the business."

"It was easy," Screech squeaked.

Her girlfriend moved closer, shutting Star out. "How modest."

"Not at all. It's a lot easier than you'd think," Screech said. How was he going to get out of this? But the girls *were* awfully pretty, he noticed.

A cute redhead standing behind him drifted over, too. "You're a producer?" she gushed. "Gosh.

You seem so young." She looked at him admiringly, with shining eyes.

"They call him the Boy Wonder," the blond said. "I read it in the paper. He's incredible."

Whoa, Screech thought. *Who cares about auditioning today? Producing is a whole lot more fun!*

But it would be pretty sleazy to take advantage of the situation. He shouldn't overdo it. "Listen, babes," he said with a shrug, "what can I say? It's tough being a boy wonder with a multimillion-dollar salary, a mansion, a Porsche, and a pool."

▲   ▼   ▲

When Zack came out of his audition, he heard Kelly's name being called. She passed him as she headed toward the studio. "How'd you do?" she whispered.

Zack shrugged. "I was so busy thinking about Jessie I'm not sure. It's a complete blur." He kissed her cheek. "You'll do just fine."

But when Kelly came out in only five minutes, her face was scarlet. "I blew it," she said. "I tripped over a wire, and then I kept looking into the wrong camera. I couldn't remember my own name, let alone the names of the music videos I had to introduce. I'm totally embarrassed. They told me I had the right look but I should take a memory course."

"It's okay," Zack said consolingly. "At least you tried."

Just then, the woman called Lisa's name, and she leaped to her feet. "Jessie's name is right after mine," she said worriedly. "Maybe she got too nervous and decided not to come."

"But she wanted it so much!" Kelly protested.

Lisa went off to do her audition. She was a little longer than Kelly, but she gave only a shrug when she returned. "It went okay, I guess," she said. "But after the audition, they asked me all these music questions, and I didn't know many of the answers. If only they'd asked me about clothes!"

"Jessie Spano!" the woman called.

The three friends exchanged glances. "I guess I'd better tell her Jessie's not here," Kelly said reluctantly.

"I'll go," Star said, rapidly coming up from behind them. "Maybe I can get them to wait for her. I'll ask."

Before Kelly, Lisa, or Zack could say another word, Star had dashed for the studio. Zack turned to the two girls. "I wonder why she was so crazed to get in there," he said, raising his eyebrows.

Kelly shrugged. "With Star, who knows?"

"We never will," Lisa agreed.

Chapter 13

▲ ▼ ▲ ▼ ▲ ▼ ▲

Screech inclined his head at a cocky angle. This was more fun than he'd dreamed possible. All he needed was money and fame, and girls just flocked around him! Who knew?

"No, really, girls, this body can only come from a daily workout," he said. "My secret is hopping."

The pretty blond looked at him quizzically. "Did you say hopping?"

"That's right, Nicole."

"I'm Danielle."

"Ah, of course." He turned to the redhead. "Let me show you what I mean, Michelle."

"I'm Nicole. Gosh, Mr. York, shouldn't you be in the studio? They called for you over the PA system just now."

"They did?" Screech said nervously. "Oh."

"The door's right there," Danielle prompted. Or was it Michelle?

Screech was trapped. Smiling uneasily, he headed toward the door. He opened it and went into the darkened room. As soon as he saw Star, he almost bolted out again, but then Danielle, Michelle, and Nicole might suspect that he wasn't a rich and famous producer. Screech slipped behind a screen until Star was finished. She was just telling the group of producers that Jessie couldn't make it. It shouldn't take more than a minute.

"But as long as I'm here," Star was saying, "I'd like to audition, too."

"Sorry," one of the producers said brusquely. "We only have time to see the people who signed up."

"But Jessie Spano didn't show up," Star pointed out. "So you do have time."

"Sorry." The producers put their heads together, ignoring Star, and started to go over their notes. Screech saw that Star was really miffed but was trying to control it.

"That's too bad," she said in a soft voice that had a rod of steel running through it. "My father, Gregory Craven, will be upset. He really wanted me to try out. And he's super close to his client, Jamie Wilkes. I hope they won't hold it against ROCK-TV."

Screech almost whistled out loud. Jamie Wilkes

was the hottest pop star in the country. ROCK-TV played his videos constantly. Would the producers bow to Star's blackmail? *No way*, Screech told himself. *Producers have more integrity*. He knew for sure, since he had impersonated one.

The producers' heads came up, one by one. "Hmmmmm," one of them said, "you have the kind of look we're searching for."

"And we *do* have some time," another one said.

"Actually, I know your father," the tallest one said. "I almost had dinner at your house this week."

Uh-oh, Screech thought. He started to inch back toward the door.

"You did? What's your name?" Star gave the producer her most flirtatious smile.

"Sylvester York. Call me Sly."

"Sly?" Star looked baffled. "But—"

"Miss Craven? We have the lights set up. Would you like to take a seat on the set?"

Still with a puzzled look on her face, Star moved thoughtfully toward the set. As soon as her back was turned, Screech beat a hasty retreat.

Danielle, Michelle, and Nicole were nowhere in sight, so Screech made his way to his friends. Jessie and Slater had finally arrived. But nobody looked very happy.

"Slater's mom lost the baby," Jessie told him. "She's doing fine, though."

"Wow, I'm really sorry, Slater," Screech said. "That's terrible."

Tears welled up in Screech's eyes, and Kelly put her arm around him. Everybody knew that Screech felt almost as badly as his friends did when something sad happened to them.

"She's coming home this afternoon," Slater said. "I'm going to stick close to home for a few days, but I did want to see how everybody did on their auditions."

"Not very well," Zack admitted. "You might say we all bombed."

"Where's Star?" Jessie asked. "I hope she's not mad at me."

A few minutes later, Star emerged from the studio. She saw Jessie, and surprise crossed her face.

"Jessie!" she cried, hurrying over. "I begged the producers to wait for you, but they said no way."

"Oh, well. What can you do?" Jessie said. "Thanks for trying. And thanks for not being mad at me for not showing up."

Kelly and Zack sighed. It looked like their plan backfired. Their chance to show Jessie what a worm Star Craven was had completely collapsed!

"The funniest thing happened," Star said. "While I was in there, they asked *me* to audition. Can you believe it? I was just *awful*. I was so nervous!"

"You seemed pretty relaxed to me," Screech said.

Star swiveled and saw Screech for the first time, standing next to Zack and Kelly. Her face contorted in rage.

"You!" she said, advancing on him. She looked at Kelly and Zack with venom in her eyes. "And you and you! It was a plan, wasn't it! This scrawny guy is your friend, isn't he?"

"Hey," Jessie said uneasily. "Cool it, Star. Screech is our friend."

"Screech?" Star screeched. "I'll kill him!"

Screech leaped behind Zack and peered out anxiously.

"You impersonated Sly so that I wouldn't know the right way to dress for my audition!" Star yelled.

"Not technically," Zack said. "Actually, we were just waiting to see if you'd tell Jessie the truth."

"Wait a second. Star, you weren't planning to audition," Jessie broke in, puzzled.

Kelly opened her mouth, but Zack nudged her. She knew he was right. Star would dig her own grave.

Star scanned Jessie's appearance. "That's why you changed!" she exclaimed. "You knew it was a plan to get me. You were only pretending to go along." A crafty look came over Star's face. "The thing is," she said quickly, "I must have misunderstood what Screech meant by the girl-next-door type. All that hopping makes it hard to hear, you know. And, besides, the girl next door in *my* neighborhood looks pretty hot. So when I told you that they were looking for the sexy, sophisticated type, I wasn't really lying at all."

Jessie crossed her arms. It had taken her a while, but she was finally beginning to see. "So you didn't want to embarrass me, Star? And you didn't want to spoil my audition? And the fact that *you're* dressed like a girl-next-door type today means absolutely nothing?"

"Of course not," Star said staunchly. "Are you saying that I planned to audition? It's just not true. Jessie, why would I do that?" she asked, widening her green eyes innocently. "I've been behind you, one hundred percent!"

"Hey, babe!" Thunder had come through the door and caught sight of them. He strode over to them, and Jessie winced. As if she didn't have enough troubles! But Thunder ignored her and went straight to Star. He enveloped her in a huge hug. "How was your audition?"

Star flushed crimson. "I wasn't very good," she mumbled. "They didn't seem very impressed with me at all."

"I'm sure you're being modest," Zack said.

Screech nodded. "And, besides, Star, you *know* they were impressed with your father. After all, it was only after you mentioned that he might pull Jamie Wilkes's videos that they gave you the audition."

Star's face went from red to white. She gave

Thunder a tremulous smile. "I'm feeling shaky after my audition," she cooed. "Do you think we could sit down?"

"Right away, babe."

Jessie watched the two of them walk off, Star resting her head against Thunder's muscled arm.

"No wonder he hasn't called me," she said. Then she turned to Kelly. "You were right. She was after him the whole time. I was a complete jerk, you guys. Can you ever forgive me for not listening to you?"

"Hmmm," Kelly said, putting a finger to her cheek.

"Hmmm," Zack said, pretending to think.

"Forgive you?" Lisa asked. "Like, right now?"

Slater grinned wickedly. "You mean without making you suffer?"

Jessie grinned. "Come on, you guys. Do I need to grovel?"

"Weelll . . . ," Kelly said. But she couldn't help grinning.

"I'll show you how, Jessie," Screech offered helpfully.

Jessie slung her arms around their shoulders. "You guys are the best."

"*You're* the best," Kelly said. "And you had a point. We put you in a box and labeled it JESSIE. We all have different facets to our personalities, and we shouldn't box each other in. For instance, I know that Zack is more than a schemer. He's a caring person."

"And Kelly's more than pretty," Lisa said. "She's smart."

"And Slater is more than muscles," Jessie said. "He's the most sensitive guy I've ever met."

"And Lisa's more than a fashion plate," Zack said. "She's a hospital volunteer."

"And Screech is more than weird," Kelly said. "He's—"

Lisa gave her a look. "Don't push it," she said.

Everyone laughed. "Well, I know one thing for sure," Jessie said. "I'm glad that that devious Star is just a memory."

"She'll never bug us again," Zack agreed.

"Attention, everyone!" Sly York—the *real* Sly York—came out of the studio. "It's time to announce the winners of the VJ for a Week Contest."

The buzz of conversation in the room stopped immediately. Everyone turned toward Mr. York and held their breaths.

"The producers are proud to announce that the week-long VJs will be . . . for the boys, Zack Morris!"

Kelly let out a squeal and hugged Zack.

"And . . . Star Craven!"

Zack, Kelly, Jessie, Slater, and Screech were frozen with shock. They exchanged horrified glances. It looked like they hadn't seen the last of the devious Star after all. Not by a long shot!

Don't miss the next  novel about the

"SAVED BY THE BELL" gang

ZaCK'S LaST SCaM

While Zack and his gorgeous co-anchor Star Craven are heating up the ROCK-TV set with their steamy chemistry, Kelly is losing her cool! Can Zack be a big star *and* hold onto Kelly forever? And can Lisa ever get super-hunk Cal Everhart to notice her? Find out in the next "Saved by the Bell" novel!